HEART

AN ELEMENTAL ASSASSIN NOVELLA

JENNIFER ESTEP

Heart Stings

Winter's Web

To all the fans of the Elemental Assassin series who wanted more stories, this one is for you.

To my mom and my grandma—for everything.

To characters like Hugh Tucker—who turn out to be so much more than just villains.

Author's Note

Heart Stings is a 38,000-word novella from the point of view of Lorelei Parker. It takes place after the events of **Last Strand**, book 19 in the **Elemental Assassin** urban fantasy series.

Heart Stings first appeared in the **Dirty Deeds 2** anthology in 2022.

1

"We're getting married—again!"

Mallory Parker, my grandmother, made that pronouncement in a loud, proud voice and followed it up with a wide, beaming smile. Me? I held back a groan and downed some water from my crystal goblet to hide the grimace twisting my face.

Stuart Mosley, Mallory's husband, must have noticed my lack of enthusiasm, because he leaned forward and looked at me. "Don't worry, Lorelei. We're not actually getting *married* again. We've already been through that whole shebang once, which was plenty for me."

Mallory's blue eyes narrowed, and every single part of her body bristled, including the wrinkles that lined her face. She sat up to her full height and somehow managed to peer down her nose at Mosley, despite the fact that they were both dwarves and only around five feet tall. "I wasn't aware that one of the happiest days of my life was a *shebang*."

Mosley reached over and squeezed her hand, his hazel eyes gleaming in his tan, wrinkled face. "You know what I mean. All the fuss around planning the wedding. Picking out suits and dresses and flowers and ten different desserts for the reception. Now, that was most definitely a *shebang*. And for the record, it was one of the happiest days of my life too. And every day since then has only made me happier."

A pleased, pink blush swept across Mallory's pale cheeks. She curled her hand into his, and the massive diamond ring on her finger sparkled like a star. The two elderly dwarves stared into each other's eyes, completely focused on the love they saw reflected in each other's soft, adoring gaze.

They were a striking, distinguished couple. With her teased, cloudlike coif of snow-white hair, powder-blue cocktail dress, and perfect posture, Mallory looked as regal as a queen. Mosley's wavy silver hair was expertly cut and styled, and his navy suit was impeccable, although his hooked, slightly crooked nose made him look more like a retired boxer than the president of First Trust bank and one of the most powerful businessmen in Ashland.

I cleared my throat, interrupting their lovey-dovey staring contest. "So, if you're not going through the whole *shebang* again, then what *are* you doing?"

Mallory pulled her gaze away from Mosley and focused on me again. "We're simply hosting a second reception, because . . ." Her voice trailed off. "Well, you know what happened at our first wedding reception."

Everyone in Ashland knew what had happened at Mallory and Mosley's reception, which had been the grand finale to their Valentine's Day wedding last month. For the most part, things had gone off without a hitch. The actual wedding ceremony had been a beautiful affair, held in a ballroom at the Five Oaks Country Club and attended by friends and family from both near and far. The following reception had featured scrumptious food, lovely decorations, and upbeat music, and everyone had been talking, laughing, dancing, and having a terrific time.

Until Emery Slater had crashed the party.

The female giant had stormed into the ballroom and taken everyone hostage. Emery and her fellow giants had threatened to start shooting people unless Gin Blanco, the assassin known as the Spider, had agreed to leave with them. And in true Gin-being-Gin fashion, she had sacrificed herself and gone with the giants to protect the innocent guests, who had included her own friends and family.

"I told you that asking Gin to be a bridesmaid was risky," I said. "Especially since she was hot on the trail of Mason Mitchell at the time."

Mason Mitchell was a Stone elemental and the longtime leader of the Circle, a secret society that had been behind much of the crime and corruption in Ashland for decades. Mason was also Gin's uncle and the man who was ultimately responsible for the deaths of her parents years ago.

"We had to ask Gin to be in our wedding," Mosley replied. "We all love her, and none of us would be sitting here right now if it wasn't for her."

True. Gin had saved my life when Renaldo Pike, my abusive father, had tried to kill me when I was a teenager, and she'd protected both me and Mallory from Raymond Pike, my half brother, when he'd come to Ashland to try to murder me several months ago. More recently, Gin had saved Mosley from Alanna Eaton, a cannibalistic vampire who'd wanted to kill the dwarf in order to regain control of the Eaton Estate, her childhood home.

"Besides, it's not Gin's fault that Mason Mitchell told Emery Slater and all those other giants to crash our reception," Mallory chimed in. "And Gin got the best of Mason in the end, just like she always does."

Yes, she had. A couple of weeks ago, Gin had turned the tables and crashed a fancy gala that Mason had thrown to celebrate the Mitchell Mile, a massive construction project that would have completely destroyed the old-timey charm of downtown Ashland. I'd fought alongside Gin that night, along with several of our mutual friends, as we'd all battled Emery and her giant goons. Eventually, Gin had faced Mason herself, and she'd finally found a way to kill him, despite his extremely powerful Stone magic.

The Spider always bested her enemies, but just thinking about how close we'd all come to dying that night still made me shiver. In an instant, the restaurant vanished, and I was staring up at the Mitchell family mansion, watching Mason use his incredible magic to rip one balcony after another off the house and toss the massive chunks of stone through the air like they were as light as marbles . . .

"More water?" A polite voice interrupted my dark memories.

I forced myself to smile at the waiter hovering beside my elbow. "Yes, please. Thank you."

The waiter poured some more water for me and topped off Mallory's and Mosley's ginger ales. He also took our food orders, then retreated.

The three of us were dining at Underwood's, the fanciest and most expensive restaurant in the city. Everything about the restaurant was subtle and subdued and whispered of money, from the crisp white linens to the gleaming flatware to the sparkling crystal water goblets. It was just after seven o'clock, so the dinner rush was in full swing. Every table was full, and folks were also crowded along the wooden bar that ran the length of the dining room.

I'd made a reservation and slipped the maître d' enough cash to get us seated next to the floor-to-ceiling windows that offered an impressive view of downtown Ashland. The Aneirin River glimmered like liquid silver as it curled past the various buildings, while the full moon and twinkling stars gilded the streets in a clean, pearly sheen. In the distance, the bright lights of the *Delta Queen* riverboat casino gently bobbed up and down on the water, like a cluster of fireflies continuously dancing through the air.

I admired the beautiful vista a moment longer, then turned my attention back to Mallory and Mosley. "So, you're basically planning a do-over for your wedding reception since the first one got ruined."

Mallory nodded. "That's right, pumpkin. And don't worry. We've already got everything booked. All you have to do is show up."

I shot a disbelieving look at Mosley, who held up his hands in mock surrender.

"Don't look at me. This was all your grandmother's idea," he replied.

I sighed, knowing that I had no choice but to give in. Despite the fact she was more than three hundred years old, and my great-grandmother many times over, Mallory Parker was still a force to be reckoned with. "What do you have in mind?"

She grinned. "Just a small, little party at the Rhododendron Inn. Nothing too big or fancy."

I snorted. *Big and fancy* perfectly described the Rhododendron Inn, a luxury resort that catered to Ashland's wealthiest citizens, along with tourists who could afford to pay the resort's sky-high prices. Given its location atop a nearby mountain, the inn was especially popular during the fall leaf-peeping season, as well as the winter months when its ski slopes were open. Even though it was nearing the end of March, the weather had turned cold again, and we'd had a significant snow a couple of days ago, with more expected later this week, which meant that skiers, snowboarders, and sledders were still flocking to the resort.

"Tell me what you have planned," I said.

Mallory grinned again, then launched into detailed descriptions of everything from the flowers to the food to the decor.

"When did you have time to put this together?" I asked.

"You've been on your honeymoon for the last few weeks."

Mallory waved her hand, making her diamond ring sparkle again. "Oh, I asked Roslyn to help me with a few things, since she did such a great job stepping in with the wedding at the last minute. Don't worry, pumpkin. Everything's done, so you won't have to lift a finger."

Roslyn Phillips was the vampire owner of the Northern Aggression nightclub and another one of our friends. She'd finished planning Mallory and Mosley's wedding after the original coordinator had gotten sick.

"We're not calling it a reception, though," Mosley said. "More like a welcome-home party to celebrate the start of our new lives together."

He smiled at Mallory, who beamed at him again. The two of them were so obviously, completely, truly in love that my own chest tightened with equal parts happiness and sadness. I was thrilled that Mallory had found someone who cared as much about her as she did about him, but I was also a little jealous that I didn't have someone similar in my own life. Hence the odd, uncomfortable mixture of pleasure and pain zinging through my body. *Heart stings*, my mother used to call such disparate feelings.

Thinking about my mother, Lily Rose Pike, made another heart sting zing through my chest, and I resisted the urge to rub the throbbing sensation away. My father had been a mean, sadistic bastard who had abused my mother and me for years before he'd finally beaten her to death right in front of me. Renaldo would have murdered me too, if not for Fletcher Lane, the assassin known as the Tin Man.

Fletcher had rescued and then hidden me in a safe house, which was where I'd first met Gin, who had been his apprentice at the time. But my father and brother had quickly found the safe house, and they would have killed me, if not for Gin. Even as a teenager, she'd put herself in danger to protect me. That was one of the many reasons I'd fought alongside her over the past several months while she'd been unraveling the Circle conspiracy.

Remembering how Gin had saved me all those years ago made another thought pop into my mind. "Wait a second. When exactly is this not-big-and-fancy party of yours?"

Mallory winced, as though she'd just been caught with her hand in the proverbial cookie jar. "This coming weekend."

"*This* weekend? As in when Gin will still be out of town with Owen, Finn, and Bria?"

Gin was taking a much-needed vacation, along with Owen Grayson, her significant other; Finnegan Lane, her foster brother; and Detective Bria Coolidge, her biological sister. I applauded Gin for scheduling some time off. If anyone could use a break from all the crime and corruption in the city, it was the Spider.

Not only was she an assassin with a list of enemies a mile long, but now that Mason Mitchell was dead, Gin was also the official queen of the Ashland underworld, and thus responsible for settling disputes between the various crime bosses, most of whom were about as mature as two-year-old toddlers throwing temper tantrums.

"Well, the four of them were at the original reception," Mallory replied in a defensive tone. "I didn't think they would mind if we had a little party while they were gone."

I snorted again. "You mean you didn't want to risk another one of Gin's enemies crashing this new party and ruining it like Emery Slater did the first one."

Mallory winced again. "Okay, fine, pumpkin. You caught me. Yes, I decided to hold the party this weekend while Gin is gone. I thought her *not* being there might lessen the risk of something bad happening."

It was a fair point. Trouble followed Gin Blanco around like a wolf stalking a deer through the forest.

The waiter returned with our food. Filet mignon with a balsamic fig reduction and garlic mashed potatoes for Mallory, fried chicken with buttermilk biscuits and black-pepper gravy for Mosley, and a chopped salad with a side of pimento-cheese toast for me.

Underwood's might charge an exorbitant amount, but the food was definitely worth it. My salad had the perfect mix of crispy romaine hearts, ripe cherry tomatoes, crunchy match-stick carrots, and cool cucumbers, along with warm lime-zest grilled chicken, gorgonzola cheese crumbles, and a honey-mustard vinaigrette that was delicious enough to drink all by itself. The thick slices of Texas-style toast were golden brown, and each one was slathered with a generous layer of rich, creamy pimento cheese with a spicy jalapeño kick.

Thirty minutes later, I popped the last bite of cheese toast into my mouth, sat back, and sighed with happiness. "Don't tell Gin, but this meal is just as good as her barbecue. Maybe even better."

Mosley chuckled. "Only if you don't tell her that Underwood's biscuits are just as light and fluffy as hers always are."

I grinned back at him. "Deal."

Even though we were all stuffed, we still ordered dessert. Mallory and Mosley split a piece of chocolate cheesecake drizzled with a warm cherry sauce, while I inhaled a vanilla-bean pudding topped with a mixed-berry compote and dusted with crumbled shortbread cookies.

I was relaxing and enjoying my post-dessert sugar rush when Mallory perked up in her seat.

"Well, well, well," she purred. "Look what the cat dragged in."

My gaze flicked from one face to another. Businesspeople, society folks, a few crime bosses. I recognized many of the other diners, but I didn't see anyone who would make Mallory sit up and take notice like that—

Hugh Tucker strolled over to the bar.

My entire body tensed, and another one of those damned heart stings shot through my chest like an arrow pinning me to my chair. Why, out of all the men in Ashland, did I have to be attracted to *him*?

On the surface, there was quite a lot to be attracted to. Hugh Tucker was around six feet tall, and his tailored dark gray suit perfectly outlined his impressive shoulders, along with the rest of his lean, muscled body. Tucker was in his fifties, but his tan skin had the smooth, ageless look that was common among vampires, and his black hair, which had just a bit of a wave to it, gleamed under the restaurant's soft, muted lights. He had high, sharp cheekbones, along with a straight nose, and a neat black goatee adorned his chin, drawing attention to his strong jaw. But even more attractive than his physical appearance was this . . . *buzz* around him, as though the air was filled with invisible admirers constantly whispering about how dangerous and intriguing he was.

A couple of women at the bar must have also heard those same buzzing whispers, because they swiveled around on their stools, like bats sensing possible prey with their echolocation. Tucker seemed oblivious to the women's admiring looks, and the vampire's white fangs flashed in his mouth as he smiled at the bartender, who handed him a glass of lemonade.

Tucker took a sip of his lemonade, then planted one elbow on the bar and looked in my direction. His black gaze trailed down my body, and I resisted the urge to fidget in my chair. I was wearing a dark blue pantsuit, along with black kitten heels, and my black hair was pulled back into its usual French braid, but his intense stare made me feel as though I was sporting something special, rather than just boring business attire. His gaze lingered on the ring on my right hand, a diamond rose wrapped in matching thorns. The rune was a tribute to my mother, as well as a symbol for how dangerous beauty could be. And me too.

My left fingers curled into the white napkin in my lap, but I stared right back at Tucker, letting my gaze slide over his shoulders and then down his chest. Heat flooded my cheeks, and I thought about how his body had felt against mine that night at the Mitchell mansion, when he'd shoved me out of the way of some falling rubble. How deliciously warm, firm, and solid he had been—and how kind, gentle, and considerate too, even with all the chaos happening at the time.

Hugh Tucker had always been a perfect gentleman with me, calm, polite, and controlled, even during the weeks he'd spent cooped up in a metal container in my shipping yard along the Aneirin River. Mason had severely injured the vampire during a battle in the Circle family cemetery, and Gin had asked me to watch over Tucker while he healed, a job that had been equal parts frustrating and fascinating.

Sometimes, when we'd been alone together, I had wondered what Tucker would be like when he *wasn't* a perfect gentleman. Part of me still wanted to find out, despite how foolish it would be. Mason Mitchell might be dead, but Tucker had been his right-hand man in the Circle for years, and the vampire was still one of the most duplicitous and dangerous people in Ashland.

Tucker abandoned his lemonade, pushed away from the bar, and strolled over to our table. My fingers curled even deeper into the napkin still in my lap, but I kept my features blank. I could also be calm and controlled when need be.

Tucker tipped his head to my grandmother first, then to Mosley. "Mallory, Stuart, you're both looking well. Married life seems to be agreeing with you both quite nicely."

"Something like that," Mosley snapped, crossing his arms over his chest and glaring at the other man.

The dwarf didn't much care for Tucker, since the vampire had been part of a Circle scheme orchestrated by Deirdre Shaw to try to rob First Trust bank several months ago.

Mallory ignored Mosley's glower and grinned at the vampire.

"Why don't you join us? We're all friends now, thanks to Gin."

Tucker's left eye twitched, but that was his only reaction to the mention of Gin. He had a better poker face than just about anyone I'd ever met, which was one of the things I found so fascinating about him. I knew what it was like to always keep your feelings bottled up, lest someone decide to take them out on you, the way my father had on my mother. The faintest slip of a smile, the tiniest hint of a disapproving tone, and the smallest, most polite suggestion were all it had taken for my father to fly into a rage and beat my mother—and me too.

So as strange as it seemed, in some ways, I found Hugh Tucker to be a kindred spirit. I'd suffered at my father's and brother's hands, just as he had suffered at Mason's hands for years.

"Thank you for the kind invitation, but I'm meeting someone for dinner." Tucker's gaze flicked back to mine. "A potential new business associate."

He kept staring at me, as though waiting for me to ask some question, although I couldn't imagine what it might be—

"Hugh! There you are!" A voice boomed through the restaurant.

Another man strolled over to our table. He was about ten years older than me, in his early forties, and quite handsome, with blond hair, brown eyes, ruddy skin, and a very square jaw. He was also a large man, several inches over six feet, and his navy suit jacket and matching shirt strained to contain his impressive physique. Both his height and his bulging muscles hinted at the mix of giant and dwarven blood running through his veins.

Tucker shook hands with the other man. "Mr. O'Neal, so nice to see you again."

The man clapped his hand on Tucker's shoulder. The sharp, jarring motion probably would have made most people rock back, but Tucker didn't move an inch. "I've told you before,

Hugh, call me Clyde." He turned his attention to our table. "Who are your friends?"

Clyde O'Neal's gaze met mine, and the jovial smile plummeted from his face faster than a skydiver jumping out of an airplane. "Lorelei."

"Clyde."

My voice and expression were just as calm and smooth as his, but I reached for my elemental magic, for the combination of Ice and metal power flowing through my body. I might not be as strong in my magic as Gin Blanco was in her Ice and Stone power, but I could still do plenty of damage with it.

Clyde O'Neal was one of Ashland's meanest, nastiest, and most ruthless underworld bosses. He was a smuggler like me, and we'd had several run-ins over the years, mostly due to us both trying to procure the same hard-to-get items. A few weeks ago, Clyde had been royally pissed when I had outbid him at an auction for a rare *Karma Girl* comic book that one of my wealthy clients wanted to give her granddaughter as a birthday present. After I had made arrangements to deliver the comic book to my client, I'd left the auction to find that someone—Clyde— had smashed the windows on my car. Petty, annoying jackass.

But I'd gotten my revenge, the way I always did. A few days later, I'd slashed the tires on Clyde's SUV while it was parked outside his girlfriend's house—and then I sent an anonymous text to his *other* girlfriend to come pick him up. The two women hadn't realized what a cheating scumbag Clyde was, and I'd greatly enjoyed watching them both scream at him from my own car down the street.

Those sorts of minor skirmishes were par for the course between Clyde and me, although he had become a true thorn in my side ever since I had taken control of Dimitri Barkov's shipping yard. Clyde and Dimitri used to work together, bringing guns, drugs, and other illegal things into Ashland—until Gin had killed Dimitri several months ago.

A week after I moved my business into the shipping yard, Clyde had come calling, trying to get me to sell it to him. I had refused, and he had been pestering me about it ever since. Lately, his attempts had morphed from bush-league nuisances like smashed windows into more serious and pointed threats about the sorts of *tragic, fatal accidents* that I could have while on the job.

I didn't know why the crime boss was so interested in my shipping yard, especially since he already owned a much larger one a couple of miles downriver, but he was *never* getting his hands on my property. Not as long as I was still breathing. Then again, Clyde wasn't averse to murdering me any more than I was to killing him, should the opportunity present itself.

Or perhaps I should *make* the opportunity present itself. Gin Blanco wasn't the only person in Ashland capable of assassinating someone, and Clyde O'Neal had already caused me plenty of problems. Perhaps it was time to put an end to him once and for all.

"Have you thought about my latest offer? If it's not to your liking, I'm prepared to increase it. I just want you to be happy, Lorelei," Clyde said, his deep voice as smooth and sickly sweet as syrup dripping all over a pancake.

I tossed my napkin onto the table, pushed my chair back, and got to my feet. Given his six-foot-plus height, I was several inches shorter than Clyde, but I tipped my chin up and gave him my iciest stare. "As I've told you before, my property is *not* for sale—not for any price."

Anger shimmered in Clyde's brown eyes, and he stepped forward, trying to intimidate me with his much larger size and obvious strength. His red-hot glare and ominous looming might have frightened someone else but not me.

My childhood had been one horror show after another, with both my father and my brother constantly finding new ways to torture me and my mother for the slightest imagined offense.

And nothing—*nothing*—the crime boss could do to me could ever compare to the agony of watching my mother die and not being able to save her. But guys like Clyde O'Neal always thought they were tougher, stronger, smarter, and scarier than they truly were. Arrogant idiot.

"You should sell to me—before something unfortunate happens," Clyde said, his voice still syrupy sweet. "Shipping yards can be such *dangerous* places. Equipment can malfunction, containers can be stolen, fires can break out. Why, you just never know *what* bad thing might happen."

These threats echoed similar ones that he'd tossed at me over the past few weeks, and I gave him a cold, thin smile in return. "If something *unfortunate* does happen, I'll be sure to let you know. Especially since all those nasty malfunctions, thefts, and fires could just as easily happen at *your* shipping yard."

More anger shimmered in Clyde's eyes. He opened his mouth, probably to spew another thinly veiled threat, but a waiter came over and cleared his throat.

"Mr. O'Neal? Your table is ready. If you will follow me, please?"

Clyde glared at me a moment longer, then jerked his head. "Come on, Hugh. Let's eat. I have a business proposition that I'm just *dying* to discuss with you."

My gaze snapped over to Tucker, but once again, his face revealed nothing. He could have been part of the brick wall for all the emotion he showed.

"Of course. I appreciate your invitation," he replied, although he never took his eyes off mine. "Ms. Parker, so lovely to see you again."

"Always a pleasure, Mr. Tucker," I drawled.

Ms. Parker and *Mr. Tucker* were part of this weird routine we had fallen into over the past several weeks. Despite all the time we had spent together while he was recuperating in

Gin's shipping container, Tucker had never once called me by my first name. I had never called the vampire by his either, not wanting to be the first one to give in to . . . whatever was brewing between us.

Tucker stared at me a heartbeat longer, then tipped his head to Mallory and Mosley again. He spun around on his shiny black wing tips and followed Clyde over to another table along the wall. I sank back into my chair, although I was still painfully aware of Tucker sitting just a few feet away.

"Mmm-mmm-mmm! That is one fine-looking man," Mallory said, an appreciative purr in her twangy voice. "Then again, I've always had a thing for tall, dark, handsome, and brooding."

I huffed. "Oh, really? Funny how I've never heard you say *any* of that before."

Mallory gave me a coy look and patted her snow-white hair. "I might be old, pumpkin, but I'm not dead."

Mosley pointedly cleared his throat.

"Although no one can hold a candle to my Stuey." She beamed at the other dwarf, and Mosley leaned over and kissed her cheek.

Mallory giggled, then whispered something in Mosley's ear that made a wide grin spread across his face. Once again, I took another drink of water to hide my grimace. I was happy for my grandmother—truly, I was—but I could have done without the public displays of affection. But I supposed that newlyweds were newlyweds, no matter their age.

While Mallory and Mosley whispered sweet somethings into each other's ears, my gaze drifted back over to Clyde O'Neal and Hugh Tucker. The crime boss was watching a waiter open a bottle of champagne, while the vampire was studying a menu—

POP!

The sound of the cork squirting out of the bottle was as loud as a gunshot. I flinched, although Mallory and Mosley were still too engrossed in each other to notice.

The waiter poured the champagne, and Clyde picked up his drink.

"To our new partnership." His voice boomed through the restaurant again, as did the sharp, crystalline *ting* of his glass clinking against Tucker's.

Over the past few weeks, scores of underworld bosses had been seen wining and dining Tucker, both here at Underwood's and at Northern Aggression and other restaurants, clubs, and bars. Everyone in Ashland wanted the vampire to join their organization so they could use his knowledge of the Circle to bolster their own criminal empires. Clyde O'Neal seemed to be the latest contestant in the Hugh Tucker sweepstakes, which worried me more than I cared to admit.

Because with Tucker by his side, the crime boss might finally figure out a way to get his hands on my shipping yard— and kill me in the process.

2

Mallory and Mosley finally finished their whispered conversation. This dinner was my welcome-home present to them, so I paid the bill, and we left the restaurant. Mallory and I stood on the sidewalk while Mosley retrieved his car from the valet.

"Are you sure you'll be okay?" Mallory asked. "You know how I worry about you in that big old house all by yourself now."

My stomach twisted at the reminder. A few weeks before the wedding, Mallory had started moving her things into Mosley's house, which was only a few miles away from the Northtown mansion I had shared with my grandmother for the last several years. I had no problem living alone, but I hadn't realized exactly how . . . *empty* the mansion would feel without her. It was like a priceless painting was missing from its longtime place of honor on the wall, and I noticed its absence every time I walked by that special spot.

Despite how much I missed my grandmother, I wasn't about to interrupt her wonderful new life, so I smiled at her. "I'll be fine. As much as I love you, I've enjoyed having the house to myself. Playing my music as loud as I want, sleeping until noon, leaving crumbs and dirty dishes all over the kitchen for days at a time. Why, it's like I'm a teenager again."

Mallory chuckled at my joking words, although her face quickly turned serious again. "Well, if you're sure . . ."

"I'm sure," I replied in a firm tone. "I'm going to drive home, make some hot chocolate, and curl up with a book in front of the library fireplace."

She gave me a speculative look. "You could always ask a friend to join you, like Hugh Tucker."

"Your attempts to play matchmaker are duly noted," I drawled.

Mallory shrugged. "You can't blame me for trying. He is one fine-looking man."

"He also happens to be one extremely dangerous man," I pointed out. "Or have you forgotten all the horrible things he did for Mason Mitchell? Like having Emery Slater kidnap me, Gin, and Bria from the Posh boutique parking lot when we were trying on dresses for your wedding. Tucker might not have been at the boutique, but he helped plan the attack, and he was there when Emery handed us over to Mason."

Anger pinched Mallory's face. "Oh, I haven't forgotten about you being kidnapped and threatened. One day, I'll give Hugh Tucker a piece of my mind about all the danger he put you, Gin, Bria, and everyone else in while he was working for Mason Mitchell."

"But?"

"But you told me how he saved you that night at the Mitchell mansion. How he pushed you out of the way of the falling rubble that would have flattened you like a pancake." She paused. "Besides, I've seen the way he looks at you."

"And how is that?"

Mallory's blue eyes twinkled with mischief. "The same way I look at my Stuey, like I just can't wait to get him alone."

I pantomimed clapping my hands over my ears. "If there is one thing I know for sure, it's that I absolutely do *not* need to hear about my grandmother's sex life."

"Then forget about my sex life, and go have one of your own," Mallory countered, nudging me with her elbow.

I rolled my eyes, but I couldn't keep a smile from creeping across my face.

Mosley pulled his car up to the curb. I leaned down and hugged Mallory, who hugged me back hard enough to crack my spine. Despite the fact that she was more than three hundred years old, she was still incredibly strong.

"Be careful. It's a wicked ole world out there. I'll call you in the morning," Mallory said. "Love you, pumpkin."

"I love you too."

Mallory hugged me again, then got into Mosley's car, and the two of them zoomed away. I retrieved my own car from the valet and left the restaurant.

Instead of driving home, I steered in the opposite direction, moving away from the downtown area and crossing over into Southtown, the less affluent part of Ashland that was home to all sorts of deadly, desperate, and down-on-their-luck folks. I followed the curve of the Aneirin River, then made the appropriate turn to go to my shipping yard.

My headlights illuminated a sturdy white wooden shack sitting next to a twelve-foot chain-link fence topped with razor wire, motion lights, and security cameras. Inside the shack, a fifty-something giant with cropped black hair, dark brown eyes, and bronze skin got to his feet, his seven-foot frame taking up most of the space inside the structure. The giant was wearing a thick blue coat over a matching security-guard uniform, and his hand dropped to the gun holstered to his black leather belt.

I pulled up to the shack, stopped my car, and rolled down my window, letting Dario Valdez, one of my watchmen, get a clear look at me.

"Hey, Dario," I called out.

He nodded. "Lorelei. Everything's quiet. You working late again?"

"Something like that," I replied, instead of admitting I didn't want to go home to an empty house just yet.

I pointed to a small TV sitting inside the shack next to a bank of monitors that showed the feeds from the various security cameras. A basketball game filled the tiny screen. "How's your team doing tonight?"

A rueful grin spread across the giant's face. "Losing like usual. Ain't that the way it always goes?"

I joined in with his laughter. Dario hit a button, and the metal gate buzzed open and slid back. I waved at him, then drove through to the other side and parked in my usual spot outside the main warehouse in the center of the shipping yard.

Lights burned at the corners of the warehouse, illuminating its plain façade, as well as the rows of cranes, forklifts, and other heavy-duty equipment that surrounded the building like metal soldiers just waiting to be called into action. Everything was quiet, and I didn't see anyone lurking in the shadows farther out in the shipping yard, but for some reason, I still felt uneasy.

A shiver zipped down my spine, and I hurried over to the door and entered the access code on the keypad. The second the door buzzed open, I slipped through to the other side, making sure that the door shut and locked behind me. Clyde O'Neal might be my main problem right now, but Ashland's many, many criminals were always looking for stuff to steal, and I wasn't about to make it easy for anyone to try to rob me.

The warehouse was an enormous, open space with a metal roof high overhead, thick cinder-block walls, and a gray concrete floor streaked with black scuff marks from all the machinery that constantly rumbled across it. More forklifts lined the front wall, while pallets covered with wooden crates, cardboard boxes, and plastic-wrapped goods stretched out from left to right, as well as marching toward the opposite end of the warehouse. Wide lanes separated the various rows of pallets, while large white placards with bold black numbers hung from the ceiling, marking the different rows and sections of the building.

It was after eight o'clock now, so the warehouse was deserted for the day, and the only sound was my heels clicking against the floor as I strode down the main center aisle.

I used to be a smuggler, just like Mallory had been before me. Way back in the day, my grandmother had made her fortune running bootleg liquor and other illegal things throughout the Appalachian Mountains, from Ashland over to Cypress Mountain, then up to Cloudburst Falls, and all the way back down again. But a whole lot more things were legal now than they had been back then, so I wasn't really a smuggler anymore, just a businesswoman who rented her shipping yard and equipment to companies that needed to move goods from point A to point B and all the places in between.

What I truly excelled at was finding and procuring items for wealthy, demanding clients. Rare wines, first-edition books, classic works of art, expensive sports cars, even more expensive jewelry. If it was valuable or collectible in any way, then there was a market for it, and I could discreetly obtain the special thing your heart desired most—for the right price, of course.

These days, I didn't move drugs or have anything to do with those who did, which was one of the reasons I was having so many problems with Clyde O'Neal. The crime boss cooked and transported meth, opioids, and all sorts of other nasty things up and down the Aneirin River, and he probably wanted my shipping yard so he could increase his distribution pipeline. I had no interest in helping Clyde expand his evil empire, so he could either give up or get dead. The only question was how many more headaches he was going to cause me in the meantime. My guess? Plenty.

By this point, I was near the center of the warehouse. In addition to the numbered placards overhead, clipboards and tablets hung on metal racks at the ends of many of the aisles, and I stopped and checked several of the boards and electronic devices, pulling up manifests and making sure that all the crates, boxes, and goods were in their proper places.

Most of my employees had worked for me for years, like Dario, but random checks helped keep folks honest. Given the right circumstances, even the most decent person could be tempted to slip a box of designer handbags into the trunk of their car to resell on the sly. But mostly, I was concerned about the not-so-decent people I so often had to deal with.

A few weeks ago, Clyde had bribed a couple of my newer employees to swipe a crate that contained several rare bottles of wine that I'd spent months collecting for a client. The workers had loaded the crate on a forklift and thought no one would notice them trying to leave the shipping yard with it. Dario and I had caught them at the main gate, but the idiots had panicked and accidentally crashed the forklift into one of the shipping containers, destroying the crate and the hundreds of thousands of dollars' worth of wine inside. Which was yet another reason for me to eliminate Clyde O'Neal before he cost me any more time or money.

But according to my persual, everything was where it should be, so I moved past the pallets, goods, and racks and headed to the very back of the warehouse.

Dimitri Barkov, the previous owner, had only the most spartan and utilitarian of offices, but I preferred to be comfortable while working, so I'd cordoned off a large space and turned it into a suite of rooms, including a bedroom with an attached bathroom.

I entered the code on another keypad, yanked the door open,

and moved into the space beyond. A wooden desk featuring a monitor and a landline phone squatted on one side of the room, while several chairs lined the other side. During the day, Karlotta Valdez, Dario's wife and my personal assistant, would be sitting at the desk, taking calls and shepherding people in and out of my office. Karlotta was fond of orchids, and several of the delicate, colorful flowers perched in pots on her desk, as well as on the shelves that lined one of the walls.

I strode through that area, opened another door, and headed into my office. Actually, it was still Dimitri Barkov's office, since the space hadn't been remodeled yet. A metal desk, a couple of chairs, some battered filing cabinets. I was thoroughly sick of looking at the dead crime boss's ugly, outdated furniture, but I only had to endure it for a few more days. Next week, Vaughn Construction, my renovation crew, would start working their magic on the office, as well as the waiting room outside—

Smack!

My knee clipped the edge of one of the filing cabinets. Pain shot up my leg even as a curse spewed out of my mouth. I hopped around, trying to walk off the injury, and glared over at the offending piece of furniture. For some reason, that filing cabinet jutted out from the wall a few inches farther than all the others, and I'd banged my knee into it more than once. Yet another reason I couldn't wait to start remodeling, get some new furniture, and finally turn the office into my own space.

I hobbled over to the desk, dropped down into the chair, and massaged the sting out of my knee. A mountain of manila folders was stacked in a neat pile in the center of my desk, along with a pink sticky note from Karlotta: *Next round of interviews scheduled!*

I groaned at the reminder of yet another thing on my never-ending to-do list.

Jack Corbin had been my right-hand man for several years,

until he'd taken a bribe and set me up to be murdered by Raymond. I'd killed Corbin for betraying me, but I hadn't hired anyone to take his place in my organization yet. Hard to bring someone new into the fold when the last guy had stuck the proverbial knife in your back. Then again, I'd always had a difficult time trusting folks, thanks to my issues with my father and my brother.

I didn't have the patience to review the résumés tonight, so I shoved the folders off to the side and cracked open my laptop. I didn't consider myself to be a night owl, but I almost always got more accomplished in the evening, rather than during the day when people, phone calls, and emails constantly interrupted me. So I dove into the actual paperwork littering my desk, as well as the electronic files on my laptop.

Maybe it was weird, but I actually enjoyed bidding on auction items, tracking shipments, and all the other dozens of little details that made up my business. Clicking through online catalogs and dealing with calm, quiet numbers was a nice respite after a day of listening to outrageous demands by my clients, many of whom had far more money than common sense.

Like the woman in Snowline Ridge, Colorado, who wanted me to buy and then ship her some exotic animal that she'd seen in a tourist attraction in Cloudburst Falls, West Virginia. Or the man in Bigtime, New York, who wanted a rare mythology book from a private academy in Cypress Mountain, North Carolina, even though the academy's library wasn't open to the public and didn't lend or sell its books to anyone. Or the folks at the mysterious Section 47 Corporation in Washington, D.C., who wanted a dozen of the biggest, strongest silverstone safes that money could buy. And those weren't even the craziest things people had asked me for this week.

Sometimes I thought I should become an assassin like Gin Blanco. Because killing people like the Spider did would be a whole lot easier and much less stressful than trying to make them *happy*.

My thoughts drifted back to my father. Like many of my clients, Renaldo Pike had had more money, houses, and cars than he knew what to do with, but he'd still never been happy— unless he was hitting my mother and me.

I'd never understood what had driven my father to abuse us. Renaldo didn't drink or do drugs, and his own childhood growing up in a wealthy family had seemed normal enough. Renaldo had certainly never wanted for food or shelter or money or anything else that might make someone do such hurtful, hateful things to the people he supposedly loved. No matter how many times I thought about it, I always came to the same conclusion: my father had just been a mean, sadistic bastard who liked to hit people. Maybe it had made him feel powerful or strong or something like that. I didn't know, and most of the time, I didn't care. Not anymore.

Not since Gin had killed him.

I still remembered the exact moment when Gin had shoved Renaldo and he'd fallen backward onto the old-fashioned mace that was his favorite weapon. The wet, heavy *thwack* of the spikes punching into his back. The scream and the blood that had spewed out of his mouth. The shock and disbelief on his face. The dark, malicious satisfaction that had filled my heart when I realized that he was *dead*, that he could never hurt me ever again—and the deep, aching bitterness of knowing that my mother was still gone, that he'd already taken her away from me, and that nothing could ever bring her back.

I'd felt the same mix of emotions when I'd killed Raymond, my half brother.

Raymond had come to Ashland to murder me with his powerful metal magic, but Gin had helped me get the better of him. Together, along with some of our other friends, Gin and I had lured Raymond to the Ashland Botanical Gardens, where there wasn't very much metal he could use against us. But my brother had escaped our trap and almost killed Gin before I'd shot him with an elemental Ice gun.

The thing I remembered most from that night was the overwhelming sense of relief that it was *finished*. That Raymond was as dead as Renaldo was and that he could never come after me, Mallory, or anyone else I cared about ever again. For the first time in my life, I had finally been *free* of both my father and my brother, if not all the awful things they'd done to me and my mother. Then again, just about everyone in Ashland had something in their past that haunted them. My memories were just making me a little more melancholy than usual tonight—

A bright sparkle of diamonds caught my eye, and I realized that I was twisting my rose-and-thorn ring back and forth on my finger, something I often did whenever my mind wandered back into the past. I let out a tense breath and forced myself to release the ring. My gaze skipped over to some framed photos perched on the corner of the desk, a recent picture of Mallory and me grinning during her and Mosley's wedding and an older image of me and my mother sitting on a park bench.

In the picture, Lily Rose was smiling wide, but her blue eyes were dim, her face was pale, and her shoulders were stiff with tension, as if she knew that the peaceful moment captured in the photo was nothing more than a brief respite from my father's temper. Lily Rose had tried to leave Renaldo, multiple times, but he always found us and dragged us back.

I traced my fingers over the curve of her cheek, the glass cold and slick against my skin. "I wish you were still here with me," I whispered.

All the light in my mother's eyes seemed to vanish, and her smile faded, almost as if she could hear me from wherever she was in the afterlife and was just as sorry as I was that we weren't together anymore. Another bittersweet heart sting zinged through my chest. I tried to massage it away, just like I had the pain in my knee, but it didn't work.

It never did.

Still, I didn't want to sit here, stare at my mother's face, and lament what I had lost. I had already done that more times than I cared to remember, so I closed my laptop, shot to my feet, and stalked toward the door—

Smack!

Once again, I slammed into that stupid filing cabinet, and more pain shot through my leg. In an instant, my left knee was throbbing as badly as my right one had earlier. I cursed and hobbled forward, but for once, I didn't mind the pain.

It helped distract from the aching hollowness in my heart.

3

My knee kept throbbing, but I left my office, locked all the doors behind me, and stepped out into the chilly night air.

Instead of heading back to my car, I plunged deeper into the shipping yard, striding past the forklifts and other equipment and moving along the rows of containers that were stacked up like oversize building blocks two and three stories above my head. During the day, the metal containers would show their true colors of rusty red, burnt orange, and mustard yellow, although tonight the moonlight painted them all a dull, gloomy gray.

Numbered placards topped metal stakes that were driven into the ground at the end of each row of containers. I pulled up the list of the latest arrivals on my phone and stalked down a few of the aisles, making sure everything was where it was supposed to be. But just like inside the warehouse, all the containers were in their proper places.

I could have gone back to my car, but I was still feeling restless, so I kept walking until I reached the back of the shipping yard, where a lone container stood underneath a towering maple tree. This container was dented in several places, as though it had been dropped on its sides one too many times and was no longer in service, but it had gotten plenty of use lately.

The container was unlocked, so I swung the door open, stepped inside, and turned on the string of bare bulbs hanging on one of the walls. A table and some chairs, a cot with a pile of folded blankets, a TV, a radio, an old milk crate full of books. Everything looked the same as the last time I'd been in here, but an aura of stillness permeated the space, something that saddened me more than I'd thought possible.

Because Hugh Tucker was gone.

Given how loudly Tucker had complained while he'd been recuperating in here, he probably never wanted to see this place again, and rightly so. Even I'd gotten sick of the shipping container, and I hadn't spent nearly as much time in here as he had.

But as my gaze drifted over to the cot, memories of Tucker filled my mind. How thin and deathly pale he'd looked in the beginning. How his shoulders had slumped with exhaustion after the smallest movement. How he'd struggled to do every little thing for himself instead of asking me for help. How his black gaze had found mine time and time again. How the heat shimmering in his eyes had made all sorts of emotions crackle like live wires deep inside my own body.

I had spent hours in here, ostensibly keeping an eye on Tucker in case he needed anything—or tried to escape. The vampire's body might have been weak, but his mind and especially his tongue had been as sharp as ever. Sometimes we would snark at each other, playing our weird little flirting game. Other times I would type away on my laptop, working on invoices and the like, while he would sit on the cot and read one of the books I'd brought from my personal library to help him pass the time while he healed.

Often, when he came to a particularly good passage, Tucker would read it aloud, although I'd never known if he was reading to himself, or to me, or to both of us. Either way, he had one of the sexiest voices I'd ever heard, with just a hint of a Southern drawl softening his crisp, polished tone, and he took the time to make all the characters and situations come to life. His low, silky voice had echoed through the container, becoming more and more appealing with each line he read, and more than once I'd stopped typing, completely absorbed in the hypnotic cadence of his words . . .

I shook myself out of my unwanted thoughts. That version of Hugh Tucker was long gone, if it had ever even truly existed, and he was never coming back here—unless he tried to kill me, something that was a distinct possibility.

You didn't hire someone like Tucker to do your accounting. No, the vampire was sly, clever, strong, and ruthless, and he would no doubt excel in any role he chose to take in the Ashland underworld moving forward. I had no idea why he was meeting with someone as petty, cruel, and obnoxious as Clyde O'Neal, though. Tucker should be starting his own crew, not playing second fiddle to someone else like he had to Mason Mitchell and the other Circle members for so long.

I huffed. Instead of procuring mint-condition comic books and other expensive items, maybe I should hire myself out as a life coach. "Life Lessons with Lorelei" or some such nonsense. It was always easier to tell someone else what to do, rather than doing such things yourself.

Life lessons aside, this container was just a metal box now. Tucker was the one who had given it life, warmth, and interest, and without him, there was nothing noteworthy about it at all—except for the fact that I was standing in here mooning about the mercurial man who used to occupy it.

I sighed, although the cold metal walls quickly soaked up the soft, lonely sound. Oh, yes. The container was simply another empty space, just like Mallory's bedroom at our mansion. Mallory and Mosley. Gin. Even Tucker. Everyone else was moving on with their lives, having all these fresh starts, but I was still the same old Lorelei Parker, as deeply entrenched in my routines as this container was stuck in the mud.

Anger erupted in my chest, burning through the weary resignation and icy numbness that had gripped me. I might be stuck in place, but I didn't have to be stuck in *this* place. Not anymore. And I most definitely didn't have to keep mooning over Hugh Tucker.

Disgusted with myself for thinking about him yet again, I slapped off the lights, slammed the door shut behind me, and stalked away from the shipping container.

I said good night to Dario, drove home, and finally did what I'd told Mallory I was going to do all along: take a long, relaxing bath, make some hot chocolate, and curl up with a book in front of the library fireplace.

Tonight's read was a noir private detective story that Bria Coolidge had chosen for the book club I was in with her, Gin, Roslyn Phillips, and some of our other friends. Bria was a police detective herself, and she always picked the sort of book where femmes fatales did bad, bad things, everyone had an ulterior motive, and you could almost see the dense fog cloaking the landscape and hear the moody soundtrack wailing in the background. As if we all didn't already get enough of those things in Ashland on a daily basis. Still, the story was entertaining enough, although I had guessed who the killer was and most of what was going to happen about one hundred pages in.

An hour later, I finished the book and went to bed. Despite the hot chocolate and plethora of marshmallows I'd consumed, my sugar rush quickly faded away, and I drifted off to sleep, thinking how much better the detective story would have been if Hugh Tucker had been reading it to me . . .

Crack!

The sharp, loud, unexpected noise made me sit bolt upright in bed. My gaze darted around my room, and my heart leaped up into my throat. What was that?

I listened, but no other sounds disturbed the dark quiet. Still, something had woken me, and I wasn't going to be able to sleep until I figured out what it was. So I got out of bed, grabbed my phone, threw on a thick plush robe, and shoved my feet into some fleece-lined boots. Then I went over to the small freezer in the corner of my bedroom, opened it, and drew out a gun made entirely of elemental Ice.

Gin Blanco was one of the most powerful elementals in Ashland, able to shower people with clouds of Ice daggers or blast bricks out of a wall with her Stone magic and pelt people with the resulting shrapnel. Just like Gin, I was also gifted in two areas, but my Ice and metal magic were both much weaker than her raw power, so I needed to be far more creative if I wanted to hurt someone with my magic. Hence the Ice gun.

My mother had been an Ice elemental, and when I was a kid, Lily Rose had shown me how to make all kinds of things with my power, from bouquets of Ice flowers to brighten my room to intricate crowns to top my dolls' heads to glittering ornaments to hang on our Christmas tree. Using my magic in such a precise way had helped give me a sense of control I had desperately needed back then, especially since my father and my brother and their tempers had been so out of control.

As an adult, I'd further honed and refined my skills, making Ice guns, knives, and other weapons, which I stored in various freezers throughout my mansion, as well as in my warehouse. The chill of the gun barrel soaking into my palm immediately made me feel better, calmer, stronger—and ready to deal with whoever might be creeping around my house in the middle of the night.

With my Ice gun in hand, I left my bedroom and tiptoed down the hallway, careful to avoid the creaky floorboards in the middle of the corridor. I glanced out the windows, but the security lights burning at the corners of the mansion didn't reveal anyone outside, so I kept going and eased down the stairs to the ground floor. Gin Blanco wasn't the only one with enemies, and plenty of folks would love to see me dead for deals gone wrong over the years.

I reached the first floor and continued my circuit through the mansion, stopping to peer out all the windows. I still didn't see anything suspicious, so I reached out with my magic—my metal magic.

Most people didn't realize it, but metal was all around us, and most folks had a piece or two of it on them at all times. Why, you could hardly find a pair of jeans without a metal zipper or a pair of boots without metal eyelets to hold the laces in place. Not to mention the iron and other metals flowing through a person's blood.

I could sense, reach out, and manipulate all that metal, just like my father and my brother could, although I'd never been as strong in my power as they had been in theirs. But you didn't have to be strong to kill someone with magic—just skillful— and I was definitely that, thanks to my mother's lessons and my own adult experiments.

I didn't sense any metal in the mansion that shouldn't be here, which meant that if someone was lurking around, then they were outside. So I plodded downstairs to the basement and stepped into a concrete tunnel. This space used to be an old root cellar, although several years ago, I'd had it expanded, lengthened, and transformed into a tunnel that ended in a set of stairs about two hundred feet away from the back of the mansion. I crept up the stairs and reached out with my magic again, but I still didn't sense any unusual metal nearby, so I opened the locked trapdoor and slipped outside.

Nothing but night greeted me, and I softly shut the trapdoor and headed into the woods that ringed the mansion. Thick drifts of snow still dotted the ground from the recent storm, crusting the trees and branches in a beautiful crystalline sheen. I stepped forward, grimacing as my boots *crunch-crunched* through a patch of ice. If anyone was out here, they had probably heard that, but I tightened my grip on my gun and moved forward.

I moved from one tree to another, doing a wide circle around the mansion. The night remained cold and quiet, and no birds or animals flew or scurried around to disturb the peace, but I still felt like someone was watching me. So I kept going, determined to find them before they did something horrible to me.

I had just reached the edge of the backyard patio when I spotted a telltale stain that didn't match the rest of the pristine landscape.

The stain was dark and ugly, like old, dirty oil from a junker car that had leaked all over the clean white snow. I frowned. What was that? And what could have possibly made it?

I still didn't see or hear anything else out of the ordinary, so I crept onto the patio and crouched down behind some chairs. Everything remained as quiet as before, so I eased around the chairs, leaned forward, and dipped my hand into the dark spot. A familiar, warmish wetness coated my fingers, and I lifted them up into the beam of a nearby security light.

Blood glistened a sinister red on my skin.

I froze and glanced around again. Everything remained as calm and quiet as before, so I studied the stain again. It was only a small pool, and I couldn't tell if the blood had been left behind by a wounded animal—or a person.

In addition to the blood, some of the snow had been disturbed, and one of the patio flagstones was cracked, as though something had slammed into it with exceptional force—like a person's head.

A cold trickle of unease slid down my spine, but I wiped my fingers off in the snow, then grabbed my phone out of my robe pocket and turned on the flashlight app. I shone the light back and forth, and back and forth, until I found what I was looking for.

More blood.

With my phone in one hand and my elemental Ice gun in the other one, I followed the drops of blood across the patio and into the backyard. The blood trail led straight into the woods, along with a path of scuffed snow, and I cautiously crept from one tree to the next.

If someone was lurking out here with a gun, then I was basically painting a giant bull's-eye on my chest, especially since I was still using my phone as a flashlight. Then again, if someone was lurking out here, they probably would have shot me by now. Either way, I wanted to know exactly who— or what—had been so close to my house, so I kept moving forward—

I rounded another tree and almost tripped over someone.

A blond man with pale skin was sitting on the ground, with his legs tucked underneath him and his back resting up against a fallen log, almost like he was taking a nap, as ridiculous as that would have been on this cold, snowy night. The man's head was turned in my direction, and I froze, thinking he was staring straight at me.

It took me three long, excruciating seconds to realize he was dead.

The man might be looking in this direction, but he wasn't seeing me—or anything else. His brown eyes were fixed and still, his mouth was gaping wide, and his body was contorted at an awkward angle. I crept closer and focused my phone flashlight on him. From this angle, he looked normal, if dead.

But as I circled around, I noticed that the other side of his head was a bloody mess, probably from where he had hit the patio flagstone.

But there was one thing I didn't see: his accomplice.

This guy might have slipped, fallen, and hit the patio all on his own, but you didn't just get up and walk away with that sort of gruesome head wound. No, someone *else* must have dragged the guy into the woods, either to try to help him escape or in a poor attempt to hide his body.

I glanced around again, but the path of scuffed snow ended here. I still didn't see anyone, so I set my Ice gun down on the ground and searched the dead man. He wasn't carrying a wallet or a phone, and he didn't have so much as a stick of gum tucked in the pockets of his jeans.

He did have a gun, though.

The weapon was nestled in the right pocket of his black overcoat, but it was just a simple revolver. There was nothing special or noteworthy about the gun, other than its cheesy pearl grip, which would have been right at home in that noir detective book I'd finished reading earlier. But the weapon, along with the lack of identification and any personal effects, practically screamed *Hello! Criminal here! I don't want to be identified if I get captured or killed!*

I used the sleeve of my robe to hold the gun out so I could take a picture of it with my phone, then slid it back into the guy's coat pocket. I also propped him back up the way I'd found him and took several photos of his face. Maybe one of my friends would be able to tell me who this guy was and, more important, who had sent him here.

My money was on Clyde O'Neal, especially given our little run-in at Underwood's earlier, but the dead guy could have worked for any number of underworld bosses. Or maybe he'd been an entrepreneur, a solitary burglar trolling through Northtown looking for a mansion to rob and not caring if he had to shoot the owner in the process. No way to tell for sure.

By this point, I'd been outside for the better part of an hour, and the late-winter chill had chapped my cheeks, snaked through my robe, and plunged down into my boots. I might be an elemental, but I'd had enough of the cold for one night, so I grabbed my Ice gun off the ground and got to my feet.

I thought about calling Xavier, Bria Coolidge's partner on the police force, but it was late, and I didn't want to interrupt his night, especially since nothing bad had actually happened, at least not to me. The dead guy certainly wasn't going anywhere, so I decided to leave him in the woods.

Still, as I trudged through the trees and headed back toward the mansion, I couldn't shake the feeling that someone else was out here.

Someone who was very much alive—and watching me.

✲ 4 ✲

I returned to bed, although every faint *creak* of the mansion settling and every soft *crack* of an icicle plunging off the roof made me get up and peek out the windows again, wondering if more guys with guns were creeping around my backyard. But nothing happened, and I finally managed to get a few hours of fitful sleep. By the time I got up, took a shower, and dressed, it was almost ten o'clock in the morning.

I should have grabbed a blueberry granola bar and gone straight to work, but I kept wondering if the dead guy might have dropped something or left some other clue behind that I'd missed in the dark. So I donned a royal-blue fleece jacket, along with matching gloves, and a toboggan topped with a poofy, jaunty ball, grabbed an Ice gun, and tromped back out into the woods. I rounded the fallen log, my gaze zooming over to where I'd found the body—

The dead guy was gone.

I frowned, wondering if I was in the right spot, but blood-stains dotted the snow in front of the fallen log, looking like scarlet berries encased in the ice. The mystery man had definitely been here last night, and he had most definitely been dead, which meant one troubling thing.

Someone had moved him.

But who? And why? And when?

I scanned the ground, and I finally noticed something new: drag marks. Deep grooves cut through the snow and underlying leaves, as though someone had grabbed the dead guy by his arms and hauled him away. Curious, and more than a little wary, I followed the marks, which led even deeper into the woods.

The grooves churned through the snow and leaves for several hundred feet before the trees gave way to a grassy shoulder and then a two-lane road. The drag marks stopped at the edge of the pavement, indicating that someone had put the dead guy into a vehicle and driven away with him.

My questions remained the same: who, why, and when?

But standing by the side of the road wasn't doing me any good, so I decided to go someplace where I might get some answers.

I returned to the mansion, grabbed my purse and gear for the day, and left. Thirty minutes later, I parked my car on one of the downtown side streets and walked around the block to my destination. An enormous sign of a pig holding a platter of food hovered over a brick storefront, inviting folks to come on inside and get something to eat. Even out here on the sidewalk, a mouthwatering mix of cumin, black pepper, and other spices seasoned the air, making my stomach rumble in anticipation.

I pulled the door open, and a silver bell merrily chimed out my arrival. Heat blasted over my body, but I welcomed the cozy warmth, given the chilly air outside. Blue and pink vinyl booths lined the storefront windows, while matching blue and pink pig tracks snaked across the floor. Tables and chairs squatted in the middle of the open space, and a long counter lined with stools ran along the back wall. Everything looked the same as always, and the familiar furnishings comforted me, especially given the dead guy's disappearing act earlier this morning.

The Pork Pit was one of the most popular restaurants in Ashland, due to its great food, its reasonable prices, and the notoriety of its owner, Gin Blanco. Since Gin was on vacation, the crowd was quite a bit smaller than usual, and I didn't see any underworld bosses chowing down on a barbecue pork sandwich or sipping a sweet iced tea at one of the booths or tables. Good. I didn't want an audience for this visit.

I strode over to the counter and sat down on a stool next to a fifty-something man with gray hair and eyes and bronze skin. He was wearing a tailored gray suit with a matching shirt and striped tie, and his black wing tips gleamed as though he'd just polished them this morning. A mug of hot chocolate wisped up steam by his right elbow, and the rich, dark scent made my stomach rumble again.

"Hey, Lorelei." Silvio Sanchez nodded at me, then went right back to looking at his tablet.

Silvio was Gin's personal assistant, and I'd never seen him without some sort of electronic device in his hand. The vampire buried his nose in his phone and his tablet the way I did in a new auction catalog or a really good book.

A hand slapped a white paper napkin down onto the counter, and I glanced up to find a dwarf staring at me. She was a little over five feet tall, with a thick, muscled body. She looked to be around my age, early thirties, although I knew she was more than a hundred years old. Neon-blue streaks shimmered in her short black hair. The same neon-blue shadow and liner rimmed her black eyes, while dark blue gloss made her lips pop in her pale face. She was wearing a blue work apron patterned with tiny black skulls over a black T-shirt and matching jeans and boots.

"Hey, Lorelei. What can I get you?" Sophia Deveraux rasped in her low, cracked voice.

Sophia was the head cook and ran the Pork Pit whenever Gin was out doing dangerous, Spider-related things. Or on vacation, like she supposedly was right now. I had my doubts about that, though. Gin Blanco wasn't the kind of person who could go somewhere and just *relax*. Not with everything she'd been through over the years. Then again, I had the same problem relaxing myself.

"I'll take a blackberry lemonade for starters," I replied. "And perhaps a side of information."

Instead of laughing at my bad joke, Silvio swiveled around on his stool toward me, his gray eyes gleaming as brightly as the tablet still clutched in his hands. "Do you need something? Please, *please* tell me you need something. Hopefully to do with someone nefarious?"

"Why so eager to serve?" I asked.

He swept his hand out, gesturing at the mostly empty restaurant. "In case you missed it, things have been slow around here lately. And I'm not just talking about the lack of customers. Why, I don't think a single bad guy has strolled through the front door so far this week. Not so much as the lowliest underworld minion."

Sophia set my lemonade on the counter. I flashed her a grateful smile and took a sip. Crisp, tart, and refreshing, with just a hint of sweetness. Yum.

I took another sip of lemonade. "Things being slow is a problem?"

Silvio smoothed a hand down his tie. "Well, it's not a *problem*, per se. It's just a little . . ."

"Boring," Sophia rasped. "We're not used to people *not* threatening us. Silvio doesn't know what to do with himself."

The vampire sniffed and straightened up on his stool. "That's not entirely true. I have gotten quite a bit of work done since Gin's been gone. It's just that . . ."

"You've already run out of legitimate things to do?" I asked, teasing him.

"Well, there are only so many times I can do inventory and rearrange the storage shelves in the back," he lamented. "Especially since *some people* around here are so set in their ways."

Sophia huffed and stabbed a finger at him. "Don't you *dare* go back there and mess up my system again."

Silvio's lips puckered, but he didn't argue with her. Smart man. Sophia was incredibly tough and strong, even for a dwarf, and she could probably snap the vampire into itty-bitty pieces with minimal effort. Sophia also happened to be an excellent body disposer, so if she ever did decide to take her inventory wrath out on Silvio, no one would ever find whatever was left of him.

Sophia looked at me again. "What can I get you?"

I ordered a barbecue chicken platter with baked beans, cole-slaw, mac and cheese, and several of Sophia's delicious home-made sourdough rolls. She fixed my food and slid it across the counter to me.

Chicken slathered with the Pork Pit's secret barbecue sauce, baked beans swimming in the same brew, crunchy coleslaw with a tangy, vinegary bite, and ooey, gooey mac and cheese. I wolfed down every delectable bite, then used the soft, warm rolls to sop up the final bits of sauce and cheese on my plate. Mmm-mmm-mmm. As much as I enjoyed Underwood's fancy cuisine, the Pork Pit's down-home comfort food was a welcome treat, especially on such a chilly day.

I pushed my empty plates aside and got a refill on my blackberry lemonade. Sophia fixed Silvio another hot chocolate, and the three of us chatted back and forth, catching up on all our mutual friends, including Jo-Jo Deveraux, Sophia's sister, and Liam Carter, Silvio's significant other.

"Please tell Mallory that we're looking forward to her party on Sunday night," Silvio said after we had exhausted all the day's news and gossip.

"Of course. She'll be happy y'all are coming."

Mallory had emailed me the guest list this morning, so I'd known that Silvio and Sophia were invited, along with the rest of our mutual friends. The only folks who weren't coming to the party were Gin, Owen, Finn, and Bria. According to Silvio, they wouldn't be back from their vacation for several more days.

"So," Silvio said. "What kind of information do you need?"

Despite the fact that I'd come here in hopes that Silvio might help me, the vampire was on vacation too, and I didn't want to ruin his downtime with a problem that had nothing to do with him or Gin.

"C'mon, Lorelei," Silvio said in a wheedling tone, nudging me with his elbow. "Give me *something* to do, or I'll have to rearrange the ketchup bottles for the third time this week."

Sophia stabbed her finger at him again. "If you so much as *touch* another ketchup bottle, I will shove it where the sun doesn't shine."

Silvio blanched a little, but he respectfully tipped his head to her. "Point taken."

Sophia turned back to the stoves to fix another order, but Silvio focused on me again.

"So, Lorelei, what do you need?"

I told him about hearing a noise, finding that pool of blood, and tracking the trail into the woods. I also pulled out my phone and showed Silvio the photos of the dead guy that I'd taken. My story ended with the body vanishing from the woods and someone seemingly driving away with it.

"Well, I don't recognize him right off the bat, but it's hard to keep track of all the criminals in Ashland," Silvio said. "Text me the photos, and I'll pass them along to my contacts. I'll also send the photos to Xavier so he can run them through the police databases."

I sent him the pictures, then slid my phone back into my pocket. "Thanks. Whatever you and Xavier can dig up on the mystery man will be helpful."

Silvio gave me a speculative look. "Do you think this has anything to do with Clyde O'Neal wanting to get his hands on your shipping yard?"

I frowned. "How do you know about that?"

A sly smile spread across his face. "Well, it *is* my job to track rumors about all the shenanigans going on in the underworld. And Clyde hasn't exactly been shy about his desire to get your shipping yard, one way or another."

"No, he hasn't," I muttered. "Although I still don't know *why* he wants it so badly. His own shipping yard is almost twice the size of mine."

Silvio shrugged. "He probably wants it to expand his business. Word on the street is that Clyde has made some bad investments lately and is hurting for cash."

I'd heard those rumors too, although I hadn't paid much attention to them. Lately, my focus had been on Mallory and Mosley's wedding, along with Gin's recent heist at the Bellum Bank and then our final battle against Mason Mitchell.

But if you didn't have enough money to pay your crew and bribe the cops, then even the most ruthless crime boss could quickly go belly up in Ashland. Clyde O'Neal was a pain to deal with when things were going well. A desperate Clyde would be a much bolder and far more dangerous enemy.

I started to take another sip of my blackberry lemonade, only to find that the glass was empty. I sighed and pushed it away. "Maybe I should have gone on vacation with Gin and the others. Because right now, I definitely need a break from blood and bodies."

Silvio chuckled, and then his face turned serious again. "Maybe Clyde sent that guy to your house last night in hopes of intimidating you into selling the shipping yard."

"Maybe," I murmured. "Although Clyde usually prefers to make examples out of people himself."

The crime boss had a not-so-secret habit of beating people to death with his combination of giant and dwarven strength, then dumping their bodies in the Aneirin River right outside his shipping yard.

"I don't know if Clyde sent the mystery man to my house, but he's going to have to do a whole lot better than some random tough guy with a gun if he wants to scare me. I've dealt with far worse than that."

Silvio gave me a sympathetic look. "Of course you have."

I ground my teeth to keep from snarling at him. Silvio was a dear friend, but I always hated it whenever anyone gave me *that look*. The one that said how sorry they were that my father and my brother had been such horrible monsters, how much they sympathized with me, and especially how much they bloody *pitied* me. Sometimes I thought that look was even worse than how I'd always had to tiptoe around my father and my brother, never knowing what small, innocent, random thing might set them off.

Okay, okay, so that look wasn't that bad, but it still rubbed me the wrong way. I wasn't a victim anymore, I was a *survivor*.

Then again, when one of my friends was Gin Blanco, it was hard for folks to remember that I was a badass in my own right. Just like Silvio, Sophia, and the rest of our friends were smart, tough, strong, and capable in their own ways. But the legend of the Spider tended to eclipse us all.

Silvio must have sensed my simmering ire, because he cleared his throat, focused on his tablet again, and started swiping through screens. "I'll email these photos to Xavier right now. Maybe I can have some info to you in a couple of days."

"Anything you and Xavier can dig up would be great," I replied, forcing my voice to remain calm and even. "Maybe this guy was creeping around on Clyde's orders, or maybe he was just looking for a mansion to rob. Either way, I'd like to know who he was and especially who might have moved his body."

"I'm on it." Silvio glanced at me out of the corner of his eye. "By the way, how are your interviews going? Have you hired a new number two yet?"

The image of all those manila folders waiting on my desk flashed through my mind, and once again, I had to grind my teeth to keep from snarling. It took me a few seconds to unlock my jaw and answer Silvio.

"I have some more interviews set up with potential replacements today." A thought occurred to me, and I leaned forward and gave the vampire my warmest, friendliest, and most enticing smile. "Although I will cancel them all immediately if *you* come work for me, Silvio. I'll double your salary, give you a company car, anything you want."

I wasn't joking. I would double, triple, quadruple Silvio's salary if I thought I could steal him away from Gin. He was an excellent assistant, and he would make my work life so much easier.

He laughed and shook his head. "As tempting as your offer is, I'm happy here."

I let out a loud, overly dramatic sigh. "I know you are. Darn it."

Silvio grinned back at me, then returned to his tablet.

By this point, it was almost one o'clock and way past time for me to go to work. I paid my bill and was waiting for Sophia to fix me a to-go lemonade when the bell over the front door chimed. I didn't pay any attention to it, but Silvio glanced over his shoulder. His gray eyes narrowed, and his lips puckered, as though he had just bitten into something sour.

"Remember what I said about no bad guys coming into the restaurant while Gin's been gone?" he muttered. "Well, I was wrong about that."

Sophia turned away from the stoves to see who he was talking about. I also looked over at the door and froze, just like I had in Underwood's last night.

Because for the second time in two days, Hugh Tucker had just strolled into the restaurant where I was eating.

Tucker stepped into the Pork Pit like he was just another hungry customer in search of a hearty barbecue lunch. He shrugged out of his long black overcoat and hung it on the rack by the front door. Mesmerized, I watched his smooth, fluid movements, along with how his dark gray suit hugged his body, hinting at the hard, lean muscles underneath. Tucker was far from the first man I'd seen in a suit, but somehow he transformed standard business attire into a work of art.

Tucker's eyes met mine. The corner of his mouth quirked up, as though he realized I'd been checking him out. He prowled in this direction, and I resisted the urge to look away. The second you looked away was usually the moment when the predator in front of you chose to strike, and Hugh Tucker was most definitely a predator.

He stopped beside me and tipped his head to Silvio, then Sophia. "Well, I see most of the usual gang is here. Where's Gin? Out killing someone on this cold day?"

Silvio spun around on his stool and crossed his arms over his chest. "You know as well as I do that she is currently on vacation."

"Good for her," Tucker murmured, then focused on me again. "Ms. Parker. May I have a word?"

"Certainly," I drawled. "What word would you like? Arrogant? Inscrutable? Annoying jackass?"

He arched a black eyebrow. "That's two words."

"And yet they both fit you so perfectly."

His eyebrow arched a little higher, but he gestured over at an empty booth. "Let me buy you a lemonade. Please."

Silvio and Sophia both looked at me, questions in their eyes, but I shrugged at them. I didn't know why Tucker was here or what he wanted, but I'd play along—for now.

Besides, we weren't exactly enemies, and he wasn't stupid enough to attack me in the restaurant. Not when Silvio looked like he wanted to bludgeon the vampire with his tablet, and Sophia was clutching a tomato knife with a serrated blade that was longer than her hand.

I stood up, and Tucker held his arm out to me in a clear challenge. I rolled my eyes, but I wasn't one to back down, so I threaded my arm through his and let him escort me over to one of the booths by the windows. Tucker waited until I was settled in one side of the booth before sliding into the opposite half.

Sophia stalked over and slapped a menu down in front of Tucker, along with handing me a to-go cup of lemonade. Then she crossed her arms over her chest, making her biceps bulge, and glared down her nose at the vampire.

"I'll have a barbecue chicken platter with all the fixings, along with an unsweetened iced tea with lemon," Tucker said.

Sophia gave him another hot glare, then grabbed the menu and stalked back behind the counter to fix his food. Silvio returned to his tablet, although he kept sneaking glances at us, ready to leap to my aid should the need arise.

"Unsweetened tea?" I drawled. "That's not very Southern of you, Mr. Tucker."

Yes, it was a stupid thing to say, but those were the first words that popped into my mind, and I desperately needed to distract myself from the way Tucker's shirt clung to his chest.

"Some of us are trying to watch our intake of sweets, Ms. Parker."

"Well, I've never been one of those people. Sugar is the lifeblood of many a Southerner, myself included."

Amusement danced in his eyes. "I know. I can literally smell the sugar in your lemonade." His gaze dropped to my lips. "And on you too."

Heat flooded my body, and I resisted the urge to shift in my seat.

"You always seem to have one sweet treat or another nearby," Tucker continued. "Like that dessert you were eating last night at Underwood's. Or the petit fours you were nibbling on when we met at the Eaton Estate."

More heat flooded my body, and in an instant, my cheeks were burning even hotter than the restaurant's stovetops. Several weeks ago, I had attended an auction at the Eaton Estate, along with Gin and some of our other friends. Gin had pointed out Tucker to me, and I'd been struck by how smooth, polished, and darkly handsome he was.

"Do you remember our conversation at the Eaton Estate?" Tucker asked. "Because I certainly do."

A third wave of heat zipped through my body, but I shrugged, as though I was as cool and calm as he appeared to be. "We talked about some books we had both read. Nothing important."

After Gin had pointed him out, I'd run into Tucker later that evening, in one of the Eaton mansion's many libraries. I had found him perusing a shelf of fantasy books, and I'd been mesmerized by the way his fingers had skimmed over the leather covers, as though the books were beautiful treasures that he needed to handle with care.

I'd started to sneak away, but of course, Tucker had heard me with his sensitive vampire ears. Instead of hissing threats as expected, he had been a perfect gentleman, inquiring about what kinds of books I liked to read and which ones I might bid on during the auction. Our conversation had been strangely fascinating, especially since he seemed to enjoy so many of the same books and authors that I did.

Our next encounter hadn't been nearly as pleasant.

Tucker had been waiting at the Mitchell family mansion when Emery Slater and her giants had kidnapped me, Gin, and Bria from the Posh boutique parking lot. Despite all the threats of violence on both sides, Tucker had once again been a perfect gentleman, offering me his arm and escorting me inside the mansion. He'd even shielded me from one of the giants who'd wanted to hit me. I didn't need his protection, but part of me had appreciated it all the same.

Only a few people had ever stuck up for me, much less tried to protect me. Lily Rose, Mallory, Mosley, Gin. And then Tucker, even though he was working for Mason Mitchell at the time. The vampire had a strange sense of honor that I found oddly appealing.

Even when I'd scuffled with Tucker in the woods around the Circle family cemetery, I never thought he truly wanted to harm me, not even after I'd stabbed him in the thigh with an elemental Ice dagger so that Gin, Bria, and I could escape.

Tucker frowned at my quick dismissal of our previous conversation. I also thought a bit of hurt flickered across his face, but he was so hard to read that I couldn't tell for certain.

"What do you want?" I asked, annoyed by both my attraction to him and the fact that he hadn't told me why he was really here. "My lunch break is over, and I have a business to run."

"Yes, your business. That's what I want to speak to you about." He reached into his jacket pocket, drew out a folded piece of paper, and slid it across the tabletop to me. "I have a proposition for you."

His face was once again schooled into a calm, blank mask, and I couldn't tell if there was any hidden meaning behind his cryptic words. So I grabbed the paper, opened it, and scanned the contents.

Surprise zipped through me, and I looked up at him. "This is an offer from Clyde O'Neal to buy my shipping yard."

Tucker nodded. "Yes, it is. A very generous offer."

"So that's what you and Clyde were celebrating at Underwood's last night. You're working for him now."

Tucker nodded again.

My eyes narrowed. "You could have your pick of any underworld boss in Ashland, or better yet, start your own crew. So why work for Clyde O'Neal? He's a pompous, overbearing jackass who thinks he's bigger, stronger, tougher, and smarter than he truly is. He'll *never* listen to you, no matter how good your advice is."

Tucker shrugged one shoulder, although I couldn't tell if he was agreeing or disagreeing with me. "What's that old saying? The price was right. Clyde offered me a substantial bonus for joining his organization, as long as I can meet certain performance requirements."

"Like getting me to sell my shipping yard to him," I said in a cold, flat voice.

"Something like that."

Disbelief filled me. After Tucker had saved me from the falling rubble at the Mitchell mansion, I'd thought . . . Well, I wasn't quite sure *what* I'd thought. At the bare minimum, that he was as interested in me as I was in him. Then, later on, when Gin had told me that he was staying in Ashland, I'd thought . . . Well, once again I wasn't quite sure *what* I'd thought.

That Tucker would call me? That we might go on a date? That we might finally explore this strange attraction between us? I should have known better. Hugh Tucker was simply a duplicitous pile of danger wrapped up in an extremely handsome, appealing package. Nothing more, nothing less.

I was such an idiot.

Anger sizzled through me, scorching through my disbelief and embarrassment. I grabbed the paper with both hands and slowly, deliberately, ruthlessly balled it up, cramming it into as tight a knot as I could manage. Then I set the wad down on the tabletop and used my finger to flick it back over to him. The ball of paper hit Tucker's chest and bounced off, making him flinch.

"You can tell Clyde exactly what I think of his offer," I growled.

"You're making a mistake."

"Why? Because I won't give in to an arrogant bully who's suddenly decided that he wants my shipping yard for some obscure reason?" I snorted. "Please. Do you know how many underworld bosses have threatened me over the years? I'm still here, and most of them are not."

Tucker shook his head. "Clyde is different."

"Why? Because you're working for him now?"

"Something like that."

Even more anger sizzled in my chest, and I leaned forward and stared him down. "I don't care if you're working for Clyde. My answer is still the same: *no*. So eat your food, scurry back to your new boss, and tell him the bad news. You're good at being an errand boy."

Once again, I could have sworn that hurt flickered across Tucker's face, but it was gone in an instant. Either way, the thought that I might have wounded him made something sick and oily squirm in my gut: shame.

I knew exactly what it was like to be cut down with cruel words when you hadn't done anything wrong, and yet here I was, doing the same thing to Tucker that my father and brother had done to me. I was better than that. I was better than *them*.

I exhaled. "I'm sorry. Who you work for and how you go about it is your business, not mine."

Tucker's eyebrows shot up in surprise, but he tipped his head, acknowledging my point and my apology.

"Either way, my answer remains the same," I continued in a calmer voice. "I'm not selling my shipping yard to Clyde O'Neal or anyone else."

I slid out of the booth, got to my feet, and grabbed my lemonade. I started to leave, but the image of the dead guy in the woods popped into my mind, so I stopped and looked at Tucker again.

"And if something *unfortunate* were to happen to me, you can tell Clyde that he wouldn't be able to get the shipping yard from Mallory either. We have multiple safeguards in place to prevent things like that from happening."

Tucker tipped his head again. "Understood. I'll convey your message."

I nodded back at him, matching his politeness. "Good day, Mr. Tucker."

"And to you as well, Ms. Parker," he drawled right back at me.

I stared at him a heartbeat longer, then spun around on my heel and stalked away.

✤ 5 ✤

I marched back over to where Silvio and Sophia were waiting at the counter and plopped down on my previous stool.
I also set my to-go lemonade on the countertop and pushed
it away. I didn't want it anymore.

"Problems?" Sophia rasped, still clutching that serrated
knife and eyeing Tucker like she wanted to fillet him like a
fish.

"Tucker had a business proposition, but I turned him down."

"Did I hear you right?" Silvio asked. "Is he really working
for Clyde O'Neal?"

"I didn't realize you were such an eavesdropper."

He shrugged, not the least bit chastised. "I have excellent
hearing, just like most vampires do. Besides, eavesdropping
has become second nature. Gin doesn't tell me half the trouble
she gets into, and I need some way to keep tabs on her. Eavesdropping is one of the many tools in my arsenal."

"You know that's totally creepy, right?"

Silvio shrugged again.

I sighed. "But yes, Tucker is working for Clyde O'Neal."

"Do you need help, Lorelei?" Sophia rasped.

"Nah. Clyde has been after my shipping yard for months, and he's not the only underworld boss who's approached me about selling it. I can handle him and all the others."

"Well, if you need anything, you just let us know," Silvio said.

"Anything at all," Sophia agreed.

As tempting as it was, I had no intention of asking them to intervene with Clyde O'Neal or any of my other enemies. That would be admitting I was too weak to handle such threats myself. And once word got around that I was asking my friends for help, well, that would make me even more of a target for all the underworld bosses. Nothing brought out the sharks like the scent of blood in the water.

Even worse, it would make *me* feel weak. After my mother had been murdered, I had made a vow that I would never be weak again, that I would never let someone make me feel small and stupid and at fault the way my father and my brother so often had.

Silvio and Sophia kept staring at me, so I forced myself to smile at them. "Of course, I'll reach out if I need anything. That's what friends are for, right?"

They both nodded, not seeming to notice my tight expression or hear the blatant lie in my voice.

I chatted with Silvio and Sophia several more minutes, then left the Pork Pit.

Tucker had already wolfed down his food, paid, and exited the restaurant, but I still found myself scanning the people moving along the sidewalks. It would be foolish *not* to look for him, given that I'd just turned down his boss's offer. At least, that's what I told myself. But I had just lied to Silvio and Sophia, and now I was lying to myself too.

I was looking for the vampire because I wanted to see him again, even though I knew he was employed by my enemy.

But I didn't spot Tucker lurking in any of the alleys, and I reached the street where my car was. When I'd parked here before lunch, the area had been teeming with people and vehicles. But now that lunch was over, everyone had vanished inside to return to work, and the street was deserted, with nary a soul in sight. I didn't hear any whispers of emotion from the surrounding brick buildings, not like Gin did with her Stone power, but metal was an offshoot of Stone, and my magic often gave me a sense of sound and vibration, of people and objects moving around, like audible peals and invisible waves emanating from a ringing bell.

Just like the growing hum I was sensing right now.

I scanned the street, wondering where this particular vibration was coming from, but I didn't see anyone sitting inside a car or hunkered behind a truck, waiting to leap out and attack me. I kept walking, reaching out with my magic again, but mine were the only footsteps scuffing along the sidewalk.

Perhaps my conversation with Tucker had unsettled me more than I wanted to admit. Despite my bravado, Clyde O'Neal was still a dangerous enemy, and he had used his combination of giant and dwarven strength to pummel more than one person to death. If I wasn't careful, he could easily do the same to me.

But nothing happened, and I made it to my car without incident. I had started to reach for the door handle when that telltale hum sounded in my ears again, and a delicious vibration skittered down my spine. This wasn't just the sound and feel of another person or some metal object nearby but a particular sensation I knew from past experience. I slowly turned around to find . . .

Hugh Tucker standing on the sidewalk.

My heart leaped up into my throat with a mix of wariness

and anticipation. I hadn't heard him approach, and I wouldn't have sensed him at all if not for my metal magic. Sometimes I wondered if that was why I was so drawn to Tucker. If we were like tuning forks ringing in perfect harmony with each other, whether we wanted to or not.

"Here to offer me another escort, Mr. Tucker?" I drawled. "As you can see, I've already reached my vehicle."

Humor sparked in his black eyes. "Too bad. It's always such a pleasure to escort you, Ms. Parker."

"You do seem to enjoy playing the part of the perfect gentleman. Why is that?" I asked, genuinely curious.

His amusement vanished, and his forehead creased as he considered my question. "My mother, I suppose. She was quite the stickler for manners. I think making me follow the rules gave her some sense of control. Certainly more control than she ever had over my father, who was a mean drunk and a degenerate gambler." He paused and cleared his throat. "My father squandered my mother's fortune and greatly diminished the Tucker family's standing within the Circle."

Surprise rippled through me. Despite all the time we'd spent together in that shipping container, this was by far the most personal thing he had ever revealed. "Why are you telling me this?"

His face remained serious. "I suppose I'm hoping it will improve your opinion of me, however slightly. About who I am and why I worked for Mason Mitchell and the other Circle members for so many years."

"And why you did so many awful things on their orders."

"Something like that."

"And what opinion do you think I currently have of you?"

He eyed me. "A terrible one, given everything I did to you, Gin, and the rest of your friends over the past several months."

Tucker had done some pretty awful things to Gin, including trying to kill her. Then again, she had tried just as hard to kill

him in return. But now, despite all that, the two of them were
. . . Well, I wouldn't say *friends*. Perhaps *not enemies* was a
better term.

Tucker had helped Gin figure out Mason's plan to destroy
the Pork Pit, and he had gone along with our heist at the
Bellum Bank, when Gin had stolen Mason's money right out
from under Emery Slater and her giant goons. Plus, he had
saved my life at the Mitchell family mansion. So my opinion
of Hugh Tucker was probably kinder than that of most other
folks, including Silvio and Sophia. Then again, they weren't as
drawn to him as I was.

"People do awful things for all sorts of reasons," I replied.
"Money, jealousy, revenge. Some people even claim that they
do those awful things for love."

"Like your father and brother?" Tucker asked.

His voice was soft, his tone kind, but I still felt as though
he'd punched me in the throat. I hadn't thought the vampire
knew about my father and my brother, but the Circle had had
dealings with Raymond, so Tucker probably knew all about
my terrible childhood.

"Yes, just like my father and brother," I snapped in an icy
tone. "Tell me, did you do awful things to Eira Snow out of
love?"

For once, I'd smashed right through Tucker's calm façade,
and hurt pinched his face before he could hide it. He had been
in love with Eira, Gin's mother, for years, although all his dirty
work for the Circle had been one of the many things that had
kept them apart.

That sick, oily shame slithered through my gut again. "I'm
sorry. There I go again, making assumptions, making a fool of
myself, and talking about things I have no right to discuss."

"If I wished to discuss them with anyone, then it would be
you, Ms. Parker."

I blinked at his confession, even as his voice wrapped

around me like a warm blanket, inviting me to lose myself in that deceptive softness, to lose myself in *him*.

Tucker cleared his throat again. "But I have something else to discuss with you."

"What would that be?"

I'd barely finished speaking when he moved forward. One moment, the vampire was ten feet away. The next, he was standing right in front of me, so close that the wind made the bottom flaps of his overcoat brush up against my jeans. That same wind also brought with it a whiff of his cologne, something soft, subtle, and spicy that made me want to bury my face in his neck and just breathe in his scent.

But I couldn't do that. Not here, not now, not ever.

Still, I wasn't about to let him know how much his stupid cologne affected me, or that I was worried he was about to deliver a more violent and pointed message from Clyde O'Neal. So I lifted my chin and looked right at him.

Tucker stared down at me, and a small smile curved his lips. "Do you know what I like about you the most, Ms. Parker?"

"What?" I asked in a wary voice.

"That you are absolutely fearless."

I frowned. "Why would you say that?"

"Because here we are, all alone on this deserted street, with me looming over you, and you fully aware of all the horrible things I've done. And yet you aren't the least bit afraid of me."

A merry laugh tumbled from my lips. "Is that what this is about? I didn't agree to Clyde's offer in the Pork Pit, so you thought you'd get me alone and intimidate me into surrendering? Please. You should know better than that."

He tipped his head, acknowledging my point. "Perhaps. But I had to try."

Another gust of wind blew down the street, ruffling his black hair. My fingers itched with the sudden urge to drag my hands through his thick locks and thoroughly rumple them, to loosen his tie, unbutton his shirt, and muss him up in some small way. Maybe cracking through that hard shell and seeing what lay underneath would finally make him less attractive and appealing. Probably not, but I was so very, very tempted to try.

"You should reconsider Clyde's offer," Tucker said. "It would be the easiest, safest thing to do."

Another laugh tumbled out of my lips, but this one was more caustic than amused. "Very few things in my life have ever been easy or safe, and I see no reason to start making them that way now. I will *never* sell my shipping yard, no matter what threats come my way from Clyde O'Neal or anyone else."

"You would be wise to be wary," Tucker replied. "Clyde might be a bully and a buffoon, but he should not be taken lightly."

A third laugh tumbled out of my mouth, this one a mix of acid and ice. "I've only been afraid of two people in my entire life: my father and my brother. Gin killed my father, and I shot my brother with an elemental Ice gun. I'll do the same thing to Clyde if he keeps threatening me."

"And will you do the same to me?" Tucker asked.

"That depends."

"On what?"

"On how much you continue to annoy and frustrate me."

A wide grin spread across Tucker's face, as though I had just proclaimed that he was the most interesting person in Ashland. In an instant, he went from cold and aloof to warm and devastatingly handsome.

"So I'm annoying *and* frustrating? How lovely to hear. You continue to say the most marvelous things, Ms. Parker. I'm not sure my ego can take much more of the sweet nothings you so drolly dole out every time we meet."

The low purr in his voice made sparks erupt in my stomach, although I rolled my eyes in response. "I'm sure your ego can handle just about anything. Now, are you done delivering threats? Because I have other things to do today."

"To be clear, your refusal to listen to reason is both annoying and frustrating," Tucker replied. "You should take the deal. It's the best one you're going to get."

"I told you before. I'm not interested in any deals from Clyde or anyone else."

I stared at him for a few seconds, letting him see how serious I was, then stepped back. Once again, I barely had time to blink before Tucker moved forward again. It almost felt like we were engaged in some complicated ballroom dance, even though we weren't doing anything more than exchanging words and sharing a few scant inches of concrete.

"It seems we are at an impasse, as far as annoying each other goes," he said.

"But?" I challenged.

"But perhaps we could do something about the mutual frustration." Tucker's voice was much lower and huskier than before, the purr far more pronounced.

His gaze dropped to my lips. I'd always thought his eyes were as black as his hair, but for the first time, I realized his irises contained a few faint flecks of silver. The tantalizing glimmers reminded me of the night sky, something with just enough light to make you risk drowning in an endless abyss of shadows.

Tucker's gaze dropped lower, to my neck, and the silver flecks in his eyes vanished, snuffed out by a darker, even more intense hunger. My heart skipped a beat, then started hammering, the sensation so hard and fast I was sure he could hear my pulse pounding in my throat.

And how do *you like your blood, Mr. Tucker? Ice-cold and served in a crystal flute?* My own voice filled my ears, followed by his reply.

Oh, no, Ms. Parker. I like my blood straight from the source. It can be quite a heady *experience, when both parties are willing.*

The vampire had said that a couple of weeks ago, when Gin had brought us lunch while the two of us were sniping at each other in the shipping container. That conversation had floated through my mind almost every day since then, and right now, my entire body was aching to find out exactly how heady that experience would be.

Tucker slowly leaned forward, as though he was going to kiss me or bite me—or both. I licked my lips and eased up onto my tiptoes, my hands itching to pull him toward me so I could lift my mouth to his—

Pop! Pop-pop-pop!

Tucker and I both whirled to the side, spinning away from each other. Out on the street, a car sputtered by, thick clouds of smoke belching out from its tailpipe as it kept backfiring. I let out a tense breath and turned back to Tucker, but he had already stepped away, and his face was carefully blank once more.

Disappointment washed through me, along with more of that annoyance and frustration. Sometimes I thought I should just throw caution to the wind, kiss Tucker, and see where things led, even if he was working for one of my enemies.

He tipped his head to me. "I will convey your sentiments to my employer, although I have to warn you that Clyde will not be pleased. There may be some more . . . pointed requests on his part."

I crossed my arms over my chest, trying to ignore the cold wind that was now gusting in between us. "If Clyde comes after me, then he's the one who will end up dead. Not me."

Another small smile curved Tucker's lips. "I have no doubt about that."

More annoyance spurted through me. I couldn't tell if he was mocking me or not. "But?"

The smile dropped from his face. "But please be careful all the same, Ms. Parker. I rather like being annoyed and frustrated by you, and I would hate to see our relationship come to an abrupt, unpleasant end."

Shock rippled through me at his confession, but before I could respond, Tucker tipped his head to me again, then spun around and strode away.

Within seconds, he had rounded the corner and vanished from sight, leaving me standing alone on the sidewalk, extremely annoyed and even more frustrated than before—in all sorts of ways.

✶ 6 ✶

Despite my run-in with Hugh Tucker, the rest of the week passed by without incident.

I upped security at the shipping yard, but nothing untoward happened there, and no more dead guys mysteriously appeared and then disappeared around my mansion. Silvio hadn't contacted me with any information yet, so I still didn't know who the dead guy might have been working with or for, but Clyde O'Neal was taking my refusal to sell my shipping yard much better than I'd expected. I didn't receive any more visits from Tucker, or threats from anyone else, but the peace and quiet didn't comfort me. Clyde was probably just trying to sucker me into lowering my guard before he sicced Tucker—or someone else—on me again.

Either way, the lack of trouble set me on edge, and soon I felt like Silvio had at the Pork Pit earlier in the week. After a while, you got so used to being in danger and dealing with one problem after another that the rare calm spells seemed a little bit . . . *boring.*

Oh, I had no real desire to be in mortal peril, but at least if something horrible had happened, I would have been able to react to it and plan my next move. Waiting and wondering when my enemies were going to strike next was far more unnerving. It always reminded me of coming home from school as a kid and never knowing what kind of mood my father would be in. Whether Renaldo would be kind and charming, or cold and aloof, or angry and abusive.

As a distraction, I threw myself even deeper into work, and I ramped up my search for someone to help me run the shipping yard, along with the rest of my business. I plowed through dozens of résumés and background checks and even conducted several in-person interviews, but none of the applicants was quite right. They were either too innocent, inexperienced, and idealistic or too hardened, bitter, and jaded like me.

Even worse, almost every single person had lied on their application in one way or another, and the skeletons in some people's closets made me even more wary of them. If folks had told me the truth, I might have been able to overlook their prior misdeeds. After all, I wasn't exactly an upstanding citizen myself, and I'd done plenty of awful things. But starting out with a lie—like claiming you hadn't embezzled thousands of dollars from your last employer when you actually had— would only lead to more trouble in the end for me.

My other main distraction was Mallory and Mosley's take-two wedding reception. Despite all the preplanning my grandmother had done, I still spent several hours helping her pick out table linens, decide on a playlist, and taste-test appetizers, entrees, and desserts. So much for Mallory's claim that I wouldn't have to lift a finger. Still, spending some quality time with my grandmother helped ease the lonely ache I had felt ever since she had moved in with Mosley.

Finally, the night of the party arrived. Mallory and I had also gone shopping earlier in the week, and I shimmied into a royal-blue cocktail dress with a sweetheart neckline, elbow-length sleeves, and a flared skirt that stopped at my knees. I left my black hair loose around my shoulders, highlighted my blue eyes with smoky silver shadow and liner, and painted my lips a deep, dark scarlet. Black kitten heels and my rose-and-thorn ring completed my party ensemble. I grabbed my coat and purse and drove over to the Rhododendron Inn. A clipper storm had moved through Ashland yesterday and covered the ground with a couple more inches of snow and ice, but the winding road that led up to the resort was clear.

The Rhododendron Inn had been built in the early 1900s by Marisol Patton, a wealthy woman who wanted a mountaintop retreat so she could escape the sweltering summer heat in the lower hills and hollers around the city. Over the years, the Patton family had added on to the inn, until now the massive structure boasted thirteen stories and three wings, along with a spa, a golf course, a man-made lake, and a chairlift that climbed up to the ski and sledding slopes on the very tiptop of the mountain.

The resort's exterior featured round white stones crisscrossed with thin black wooden beams, making it look like an enormous tic-tac-toe board that had been partially filled in. Golden light spilled out of the wide picture windows, highlighting the folks in tuxedos and glittering gowns who were streaming toward the main entrance. I handed my car off to a waiting valet and followed the crowd to the main ballroom in the center of the resort.

I'd been to dozens of luncheons and fund-raisers here, but tonight the staff had transformed the space into a winter wonderland that mirrored the snowy landscape outside. Sparkly silver linens adorned the tables, while matching panels of fabric covered with tiny white and blue twinkle lights swooped down from the ceiling like elaborate electrified cobwebs. Even more lights wrapped around glittering silver trees clustered together in the corners.

Some folks were meandering along the buffet tables, while others were standing in groups, talking, laughing, and sipping drinks. An enthusiastic band was playing swing tunes on the stage in the back of the ballroom, and the mood was fun and festive. A smile spread across my face. Mallory had been right. This was the perfect way to celebrate her new life with Mosley.

"Pumpkin! There you are!" Mallory waved at me, and I headed over to her.

My grandmother looked lovely in a powder-blue cocktail dress covered with silver sequins, while her favorite diamond tiara was nestled in her teased cloud of snow-white hair. Mosley was by her side, looking as distinguished as always in a matching powder-blue tuxedo. Together, the two of them reminded me of a prom queen and her adoring king.

I kissed them both on their cheeks, then drew back. "The party is wonderful."

The two dwarves beamed at me. Mosley moved away to talk to some other folks, but Mallory looked past me as though she was searching for someone.

"You didn't bring a date?" she asked in a hopeful voice.

Somehow I managed to keep from rolling my eyes. "No, I didn't bring a date."

"Well, that's too bad." Her shoulders drooped in disappointment, although she perked right back up again. "But it's not too late for you to rustle up a date. The party will go to at least midnight, maybe longer if I have my way."

This time, I did roll my eyes. "I'm perfectly fine flying solo tonight. Besides, it's not like I can just wander around the resort, grab some random guest, and ask them to be my date."

A guilty look flickered across Mallory's face. "Well, actually, that might be easier than you think."

Before I could puzzle out her weird words, I spotted Silvio Sanchez waving at me in a clear *please come here* gesture.

I nodded at him and looked at Mallory again. "Regardless

of my lack of a date, you should mingle with your guests. Go, enjoy your party. We'll catch up again later."

Mallory's eyes narrowed with suspicion, but she headed toward Mosley and joined his conversation with a group of people. As soon as she was distracted, I hurried over to Silvio. The vampire was dressed in a classic black tuxedo, as was the forty-something man standing beside him. The second man was much taller and broader, with brown hair, blue eyes, and tan skin. Like Clyde O'Neal, this man had a mix of giant and dwarven blood running through his veins that made him extremely tough, strong, and dangerous.

Liam Carter grinned at me. "Great party, Lorelei."

Liam, another one of our mutual friends, was known throughout Ashland for providing protection services to everyone from wealthy citizens to police witnesses to criminals battling other criminals. I'd considered hiring Liam to watch over Mallory and Mosley in case Clyde O'Neal decided to target them instead of me, but I still wanted to handle Clyde myself, so I hadn't approached Liam—yet.

Besides, Liam was still recovering from being beaten almost to death by Emery Slater a few weeks ago. Jo-Jo Deveraux had used her Air magic to heal Liam's physical injuries, but I knew from personal experience that you didn't so easily recover from that sort of emotional trauma, and I didn't want to add anything else to his plate right now unless absolutely necessary.

I smiled back at him. "Thanks, but this was all Mallory. You should go tell her. My grandmother adores compliments."

"I'll do that." Liam touched Silvio's elbow. "And get us some drinks while I'm gone?"

Silvio nodded, and Liam disappeared into the crowd. The vampire watched him go, a dreamy expression on his face.

"I take it things are going well with Liam?" I asked.

"So far, so good." Silvio looked at me. "I know this is a

party, but I have some news you might be interested in."

"Let me guess. Gin is home early and going to crash the party with dozens of enemies in tow."

Silvio laughed at my joke, but his face quickly turned serious. "Nothing as bad as that. Although I did finally learn the identity of your mystery man."

He pulled his phone out of his jacket pocket, tapped on it a few times, and showed me the device. The dead guy's face filled the screen, and he was smirking in a driver's license photo.

"Actually, Xavier found out who he was," Silvio continued. "Someone left your mystery man buried under some trash bags in an alley over in Southtown. A couple of sanitation workers found him earlier today. Xavier ran his prints and sent the info to me."

"Who is he?" I asked.

"Walter Butler. He originally hails from Blue Marsh, and he has a rap sheet a mile long. Assault, armed robbery, and the like. But for the last few years, Walter has been hiring himself out as a hit man. He's suspected of being involved in almost a dozen murders for hire."

I frowned. "You think someone sent Walter to kill me?"

Silvio shrugged. "The thought had crossed my mind, especially given your recent troubles with Clyde O'Neal."

"Did the hit man work for Clyde?"

Silvio shrugged again. "Not that I can tell, but I haven't dug up that much information on him yet. I put out feelers to my usual contacts, so I should know more soon . . ."

He kept talking, but a flash of movement caught my eye, and I looked past him. Someone had darted past the open ballroom doors, a black blur that had gone by almost too fast for me to follow.

Suspicion filled me. I only knew one person who was that fast on their feet, so I reached out with my metal magic. It was hard to tell, given the conversation and music filling the ballroom, but I could have sworn that telltale hum erupted in my ears.

". . . let you know as soon as I find out more—"

"Thanks for the info, Silvio." I cut him off. "I really appreciate it, but I need to check on something. I'll be back in a few minutes."

Before he could say anything else, I strode past him and hurried out the open doors. To my left, several folks were talking and drinking, but when I turned to my right, I once again saw that black blur of movement out of the corner of my eye. More suspicion filled me, and I headed in that direction.

I smiled and nodded at everyone I passed, but I quickly left the crowded main hallway behind and stepped into an empty corridor. No one was moving through this area, and the only sound was the faint scuff of my heels against the carpet. Still, I kept moving forward, following that strange hum in my ears, wondering if I was just imagining the sensation—

A door to my right opened. I whirled in that direction, but before I could react, a hand darted out and dragged me forward, pulling me into another room. I stumbled, and my purse slipped through my fingers and dropped to the floor. That hand tightened around my wrist, spinning me around. I slammed up against someone's chest, and a second hand settled on my waist, steadying me.

I lurched back. My head snapped up, and my own hands curled into fists, ready to punch whoever had grabbed me—

Hugh Tucker.

For the third time in the last few days, I froze at the sight of the vampire.

Like every other man here tonight, Tucker was dressed in

a tuxedo, but he wore it far better than most. The black jacket outlined his shoulders, hinting at the lean muscles underneath, while the white shirt brought out his tan skin, along with his black hair, eyes, and goatee. My surprise vanished, although my heart kept hammering, picking up speed with each passing second.

"What are you doing here?" I demanded, slowly loosening my fists. "And why did you grab me like that?"

"Apologies," Tucker replied. "But it seemed like the best, easiest, and quickest way to get you out of the hallway."

His gaze roamed over me, and appreciation sparked in his eyes. "You look lovely."

I smoothed my hands down the front of my dress. His gaze tracked the movement, and a hungry look filled his face, as though he wanted to follow the motion with his own hands.

Heat shot through my body at the thought of him touching me, but I dropped my hands to my sides and glanced around. White tile, large stalls, a long counter studded with silver sinks and topped by a mirror with frosted edges.

I frowned. "Why did you yank me into a bathroom?"

"The room doesn't matter. I just wanted to get you out of sight."

"Why?"

Tucker fell silent, his lips pressing into a thin line.

I waited, but when it became apparent that he wasn't going to respond, I crossed my arms over my chest. "You're always so mysteriously quiet whenever someone asks you a direct question. It's one of your worst traits. If you aren't going to answer me, then I'm leaving."

I started to head toward the door, but he stepped in front of me, blocking the exit.

"I can't let you return to the party."

"Why not?" Suspicion filled me. "What's going on?"

"Exactly what I told you would happen," Tucker replied.

"Clyde O'Neal does not appreciate your continued refusal to sell him your shipping yard."

My eyes narrowed. "Clyde is *here*? At the party?"

"Yes, and he's looking for you. He wants to . . . further discuss the situation."

I snorted. "You mean he's here to kidnap and kill me and take my shipping yard by force."

"Something like that. Hence my escorting you in here." He pointed to a door in the wall on the opposite side of the room. "If you hurry, you can slip out that way, retrieve your car, and leave before Clyde realizes you're gone."

I lifted my chin. "I am *not* running away from Clyde O'Neal or anyone else."

Tucker glowered at me. "There you go again, being annoying and frustrating."

Anger shot through me, and I slapped my hands on my hips. "More annoying and frustrating than you luring me away from the ballroom and dragging me in here?"

He frowned. "I didn't lure you away. I was doing a discreet sweep of the area, but somehow you spotted me anyway. How did you do that? Because I excel at not being seen."

I opened my mouth to tell him about my metal magic, about this oddly pleasing hum I sensed whenever he was around, but I clamped my lips shut. Tucker wasn't telling me everything, so why should I reveal anything about myself or my power to him in return?

He arched an eyebrow. "Now who's being so mysteriously quiet when asked a direct question?"

I stiffened at him throwing my own words back in my face. "I'm not leaving. I'll deal with Clyde myself, before he does something stupid and ruins Mallory and Mosley's party."

I started toward the door, but once again Tucker blocked my path. I tried to skirt around him, but he was faster, and he countered every move I made. Anger and annoyance bubbled up in my chest like a geyser about to erupt, so I changed tactics and went at him straight on.

Tucker stepped back, but he still didn't get out of my way. I kept charging forward, and he kept moving back, the two of us once again doing a weird sort of dance. But this one ended as quickly as it began, and a few seconds later, Tucker's back was pressed up against the bathroom door, the same door I needed to go through to return to the party.

He smirked at me, knowing that I didn't have the strength to physically move him away from the door. I resisted the urge to stick my tongue out at him.

"Fine," I muttered. "Be a stubborn child. I'll just go out the other door and circle back around to the ballroom that way."

I whirled around to storm toward the other exit. I had only taken a few steps forward when his voice sounded behind me.

"Lorelei. Stop. Please."

That soft, almost whispered *please* made me pause and look over my shoulder. Tucker had stepped away from the door, although his hands were now clenched into fists by his sides. I wasn't sure what he was asking. I don't think he knew either. But for a change, one raw emotion after another flashed across his face—interest, desire, longing. All the hot, annoying, frustrating things I felt whenever I was around him.

That vibration in my ears, my body, my heart hummed even louder and stronger, but it wasn't my metal magic. Not really. No, this was just my own intense attraction to Hugh Tucker.

And for once in my life, I decided to give in to temptation, to do something fun and reckless and stupid. I spun around and strode toward him, closing the distance between us again.

Tucker opened his mouth, but I cut him off.

"No more talking," I growled.

Then I dug my fingers into his tuxedo jacket, yanked him forward, and pressed my lips to his.

✷ 7 ✷

Over the past few weeks, I'd thought quite a lot about what kissing Hugh Tucker would be like. Whether it would be sweet and soft or hot and hard. Whether he would hold me close or keep his distance. Whether he would touch me the way I longed to touch him or keep his hands to himself. And especially whether he would feel, want, and desire as much as I did whenever I looked at him.

The actual kiss itself was a combination of all those things— and then some.

The first touch of my mouth against his was gentle enough, although that small, relatively innocent contact ignited a fire deep inside me. Suddenly, everything felt a little clearer, a little sharper, a little more intense, from the press of my lips against his to the solid plane of his chest under my fingertips to the heat of his body warming my own.

Unable to resist that hypnotic pull, I stepped even closer to him, seeing how well my curves fit against the harder, sharper angles of his body. The answer? Quite nicely.

I wanted to mold my body to his, to feel every single inch of him pressing up against me, but I forced myself to remove my lips from his and release his jacket. I had no idea how he would respond, now that I had finally acted on this unspoken, undefined thing simmering between us. Maybe he didn't feel the same way. Maybe flirting with me had just been a game, a way for him to pass the time while he was recuperating from his injuries. Maybe this was all in my head.

I started to step back, to put some more distance between us, but Tucker reached out and gently clasped my hands in his. Those starry silver flecks shimmered in his black eyes, but they soon vanished, swept away by the hunger that filled his face.

"Lorelei." He whispered my name, his voice lower and rougher than before, a faint question in his tone, as though he wasn't sure whether he wanted to pull me closer or push me away.

Well, I knew what I wanted, so I leaned forward and pressed my lips to his again. Tucker growled, grabbed my hips, and yanked me toward him, deepening the kiss.

I opened my mouth, and his tongue darted out to meet mine. With every press and stroke of our lips and tongues, that fire inside me burned a little brighter and hotter, even as that pleasurable hum spread through my entire body, like a smug, satisfied purr rumbling through a cat's belly.

I wound my arms around his neck and plastered my body against his. Tucker's hands squeezed my hips, then snaked up my back. The two of us were glued together from lips to hips to thighs, and yet it still wasn't *enough*.

Our lips and tongues found each other again and again, every kiss a little longer and more intense than the one before it.

Everything else vanished. The empty bathroom. The cool tile surrounding us. The faint murmur of the party music in the distance. All that mattered was my lips and hands on Tucker, and his on me, and the desire exploding between us like fireworks spraying color across a midnight sky . . .

A door *creaked* open somewhere behind me, but I ignored

it and nuzzled my nose into Tucker's neck, breathing in his cologne the way I had wanted to for days now—

"Oh, my," a voice drawled. "I hate to interrupt such a private moment."

Startled, I spun around, even though Tucker was still holding me in his arms. I hadn't imagined that door creaking open, and someone had entered the bathroom from the opposite side.

Clyde O'Neal.

Just like Tucker, Clyde was dressed in a black tuxedo, although it didn't look nearly as good on him as it did on the vampire. Even worse, he wasn't alone. Three other men, all giants wearing dark gray suits, had also stepped into the bathroom and were leering at me.

My hands balled into tight fists, and I broke away from Tucker and faced Clyde and his goons. "I heard you were looking for me."

Clyde's brown gaze moved past me and landed on Tucker. "Yes, I was. And Hugh found you for me, just like he promised he would."

My gaze swung around to the vampire, who moved forward, as though he was going to stand with me . . .

Tucker smoothly skirted to the side, putting some distance between us. Cool air filled in the space where his body had been pressed up against mine, although it did nothing to douse the red-hot embarrassment burning in my cheeks.

"I told you she was around here somewhere," he murmured.

The words weren't unexpected, but they flew over me like a swarm of yellow jackets stinging my heart over and over again. I'd thought—*hoped*—that Tucker was genuinely attracted to me, that he was truly, fully on my side, but it seemed as though I was wrong about that.

"Yes, you did," Clyde replied. "I had no idea you were planning a little treat for yourself before we got down to business, but I do admire a man who can multitask."

He leered at me, just like the three giants were still doing. The embarrassment burning in my cheeks and the rest of my body abruptly chilled, morphing into razors of icy rage. I seized on to the emotion, using that cold, sharp pain to ground myself. "Now what?" I asked in a snide voice. "Going to try to buy my shipping yard again?"

"Nah," Clyde replied. "I'm done asking nicely. You're too stupid and stubborn to cash out and walk away, so I'm just going to take what I want. The way I should have all along."

He raised his hand, and the gun in his fingers glinted under the soft lights. Clyde grinned, thinking he was in complete control of the situation, but the weapon didn't overly concern me. I could always use my metal magic to wrench the gun out of his hand before he could shoot me with it.

After that, well, I wasn't quite sure what would happen, but I wasn't scared. Like I'd told Tucker on the street the other day, I'd only ever been afraid of two people in my entire life. My father and my brother weren't around to terrorize me anymore, and I would be happy to add Clyde O'Neal and his men to the list of my dead enemies.

Clyde waggled the gun at me. "Let's take a walk."

To my surprise, Tucker held his arm out to me. "Ms. Parker, if you will be so kind as to let me escort you," he murmured in a cool, polite voice, as if we hadn't been making out just a few minutes ago.

I threaded my arm through his, then gave him a smile that was all teeth. "Why, Mr. Tucker, I would be delighted as always."

He winced at my harsh, accusing tone, but he didn't say anything as he led me across the bathroom and out the opposite door, with Clyde and his three giants following along behind us.

We stepped into another empty corridor. By this point, we were on the opposite side of the resort from the ballroom, and I couldn't even hear the murmur of the party music anymore.

"Take her outside," Clyde ordered behind us.

Tucker opened a nearby door, and we stepped onto an enormous gray stone terrace that jutted out from the back of the resort. Several Adirondack chairs were arranged around firepits where folks could sit and roast marshmallows and the like, while a set of wide, shallow stairs zigzagged down the steep slope to a flat area that was a popular picnic spot during the warmer months. But tonight everything was crusted with snow, and icicles longer than my fingers hung like jagged teeth off the edge of the resort roof above, as well as the stone railing that cordoned off the terrace from the open air below.

Tucker led me over to one side of the terrace. Clyde eyed us a moment, as if making certain that I wasn't going to try to run, then started talking to his men. Given the wind gusting around the terrace, I couldn't make out their low words, but I doubted Clyde was telling the giants to take me back inside. More likely, they were discussing what to do with my body after they killed me.

That wasn't going to happen, and I was going to enjoy showing Clyde what a fatal mistake he'd made by targeting me. But first, I needed to know whose side Tucker was truly on. I still thought—*hoped*—that it was mine, but I could never be certain of anything when it came to the mysterious, mercurial vampire. It was one of the many things that made him so annoying, frustrating, and fascinating.

"What are you doing?" I hissed. "Please don't tell me you've actually thrown your lot in with this crew. After working for Mason Mitchell, this would be a serious step down for you, as far as bad guys go."

"I wasn't aware there were echelons of evil in Ashland," Tucker quipped.

I snorted. "Please. We both know there are *totally* echelons of evil in Ashland and that Clyde O'Neal is nowhere near the top of the food chain. So my question remains the same: what are you doing?"

"Trying to help you, despite how annoying, frustrating, and stubborn you're being," he grumbled in a low voice only I could hear.

I arched an eyebrow. "So now I'm annoying, frustrating, *and* stubborn? Excellent. Let's see if we can add a few more adjectives to that list before the night is through."

Tucker sighed and rolled his eyes upward, as if asking some higher power for the patience to deal with me. "And I thought Gin had reckless tendencies. You have her beat all to pieces, Ms. Parker."

"Absolutely, Mr. Tucker. What can I say? I tend to react badly when someone tries to bully me and take what's mine."

Clyde finished his conversation with his men and stepped back over to us. He looked me up and down, but this time, his gaze was more thoughtful than lecherous. After a few seconds of silent contemplation, he shook his head, as though disappointed by what he saw.

"I still can't believe you killed Raymond Pike."

His words punched me in the chest, and all the air rushed out of my lungs. Out of all the things he could have said, out of all the names he could have dropped, I had *never* expected him to mention my brother.

My arm slid free of Tucker's, and I swayed on my feet before I was able to steady myself. "How did you know Raymond?"

Clyde shrugged. "One of my cousins up in West Virginia was good buddies with Raymond. They used to go hunting together. Sometimes I would tag along with them."

A memory of Raymond gutting a rabbit in the middle of the kitchen floor filled my mind, and the phantom stench of blood flooded my nose, making my stomach churn. Renaldo had loved to hunt and fish, and Raymond had been so eager to please our father that he had thoroughly embraced those activities too. Hunting for food was one thing, but my father and my brother had always been far more interested in killing than eating. They had both reveled in being cruel, whether it was to me, my mother, or the defenseless animals they stalked through the woods around our house.

"Raymond used to talk about you all the time," Clyde continued. "About how he was going to track down his long-lost sister and kill her. Of course, back then, I didn't realize *you* were that sister. But when Raymond found out that you were in Ashland, he reached out to me. I gave him the lay of the land, so to speak, and told him all about you and Mallory. Raymond was so grateful for the information that he promised me a hefty reward."

"But then I killed Raymond instead of the other way around, and you got nothing," I replied. "So now you're going to kill me and steal my shipping yard as your supposed reward."

"Nah," Clyde said. "I don't want the shipping yard. I just want the diamonds inside."

I frowned, thoroughly confused. "What diamonds?"

"A couple of weeks before he died, Dimitri Barkov and his crew robbed a fancy jewelry store over in Cypress Mountain. They got away with millions in diamonds." Clyde's eyes gleamed with greed. "Over drinks one night, Dimitri bragged to me that he still had the stones hidden in his office. I was going to steal them, but then Gin Blanco came along and killed him a couple of days later. That was even better, as far as I was concerned, until you swooped in and took over the shipping yard before I could get inside and find the diamonds."

And just like that, Clyde's obsession with buying my shipping yard made perfect sense. "And once I upped security, there was no way you could sneak into the warehouse, much less Dimitri's office, and look for the diamonds."

He nodded. "A problem that I'm planning to rectify tonight.

We're going to take a little ride over to your shipping yard, and you're going to let me and my men inside."

He didn't say anything about letting me go once he found the diamonds. We all knew he'd put a bullet in my head and be done with things.

Despite the threat of my own impending death, my gaze darted back over to Tucker, who was standing apart from both Clyde and me. Had he known about the diamonds? Was that why he'd shown me so much . . . attention over the past few days? Working for Clyde O'Neal was a waste of his skills, but fucking over both Clyde *and* me so he could claim the diamonds for himself . . . Now, *that* sort of twisty scheme was most definitely worthy of Hugh Tucker's time and talents.

Hurt shot through me at the thought that he would betray me, that he would use my obvious attraction to score himself a hefty payday. It took some effort, but I iced it out, freezing the emotional roller coaster that had been rising and falling in the pit of my stomach with each new ugly revelation about Clyde, Raymond, and the stolen diamonds.

"Now," Clyde rumbled, "according to my sources, you haven't started remodeling Dimitri's office yet, which means that the diamonds are most likely still inside. So why don't you make things easy on yourself, Lorelei, and tell me where you think the stones are hidden?"

My hands balled into fists again, and I stalked over and stopped right in front of him. Then I tipped my chin up so I could look into his eyes. "Even if I knew, I wouldn't tell you a damn thing."

"I thought you might say something like that. Maybe this will change your mind."

Faster than a snake striking, Clyde whipped his hand out and slapped me. Pain exploded in my face, and the force of the blow sent me staggering to the side, but the worst part was the harsh *crack* of his hand hitting my cheek. That one sound opened a floodgate, and memories erupted out of the dark dam of my mind and spilled out into the light.

My father slapping my mother whenever she did something he didn't like, even if it was as inconsequential as buying the wrong bread at the grocery store, even though it had been his favorite kind just the week before. All the times Raymond had pinched or punched or kicked me, claiming that I had taken one of his toys without permission, when he had offered it to me in the first place. My father and my brother taking turns hitting my mother and me, even as she tried to shield us both from their vicious blows . . .

The pain of Clyde's slap slowly receded, burned away by my memories and the hot, caustic rage they always brought along with them. I'd promised myself a long, long time ago that no one was ever going to hurt me like my father and my brother had. So far, I'd killed every person who'd tried—just like I was going to kill Clyde.

Tucker sidled closer to me, as silent as a ghost. His black gaze lingered on my cheek, which was still throbbing, and a muscle twitched in his own jaw, as though he was grinding his teeth to keep from snarling or maybe even sinking his fangs into Clyde's neck.

Clyde sneered at me, as did the three giants. He probably expected me to start crying, or some such nonsense, but I'd cried myself dry years ago, and he wasn't worth such precious emotion.

So I bared my teeth at him, despite the continued ache in my face. "If you really did know Raymond, then you know what a heartless bastard he was."

"So what?"

"So your petty threats are amateur hour compared to him," I snapped. "And you're going to have to hit me a whole lot harder than that to even come close to matching Raymond's cruelty."

Anger flared in Clyde's eyes, and he drew his hand back to slap me again. In an instant, Tucker moved forward, stepping up beside me.

"If you're going to implement your original plan, then I suggest you get on with things," Tucker said in a smooth voice. "You never know who might decide to come to the party. Why, Gin Blanco herself could show up out of the blue and ruin things for you."

Clyde kept glaring at me, clearly wanting to hit me again, but he slowly reined in his temper. "You're right. Getting access to the shipping yard is the most important thing right now. Maybe Lorelei will be a little more cooperative when we drag her sweet little grandma out of the party." He jerked his head at the three giants. "Go inside, find the old woman, and tell her that Lorelei is sick in the bathroom. The second you get her alone, bring her out here."

Even more rage flooded my body, along with a healthy amount of dread. "Leave Mallory out of this."

Malice filled Clyde's face. "Nope. Everyone knows how much you love that old woman. You might be able to take a few slaps, but I doubt you'll be so cavalier when I start hitting her."

He was right. I would do anything to protect my grandmother, even give Clyde exactly what he wanted. I opened my mouth to tell him that—

"Besides, you know how things work in Ashland. You killed one of my guys, so now I need to kill one of yours in return to save face," he continued. "Tell me. How did you get the drop on Walter Butler? He was supposed to be one of the best hit men money could buy."

Beside me, Tucker shifted on his feet, as though suddenly uneasy. The motion was almost imperceptible, and I seemed to be the only one who noticed it, but it told me something important: Tucker had killed Butler.

I thought someone had been watching me in the woods that night. Tucker must have waited until I'd gone back inside my mansion before he'd grabbed Butler's body, dragged the dead hit man through the woods, stuffed him into a vehicle, and driven away.

But why kill the hit man only to turn me over to Clyde now? Once again, Hugh Tucker was playing a game that only made sense to him.

"Well?" Clyde asked. "How did you kill Butler?"

"He made too much noise breaking into my house," I lied. "He had an unfortunate accident and cracked his head wide open on the stone patio in my backyard."

Clyde grinned. "Nice, Lorelei. Very nice. Why, that gives me the perfect idea for how to get rid of you after I get my diamonds." He gestured over at the stairs. "I'll snap your neck, bring you back here, and toss you down the steps. Everyone will think you came outside to admire the view and tragically slipped on the snow and ice and fell to your death."

I snorted again. "Please. This is Ashland. The city of crime, corruption, and secret Circle societies. No one in their right mind will believe that my death was an *accident*."

He shrugged. "I don't care what people believe. Only that I get my diamonds, and you wind up dead."

I opened my mouth to snipe back at him, but he snapped his fingers, cutting me off.

"Actually, I have an even better idea." Clyde grinned again, then lifted his gun and aimed it at Tucker. "If I'm going to get my hands dirty, then I might as well kill Hugh too."

※ **8** ※

ucker tensed ever so slightly, although he gave Clyde a bored look, as if the gun aimed at his chest was of little consequence. "What are you doing? Put that thing away."

Clyde laughed, but it was a low, ugly sound. "Oh, please. How big of an idiot do you think I am? I tell a few folks that I'm getting Lorelei's shipping yard one way or another, and the next thing I know, you're calling and just begging to come work for me." He shook his head. "I've never claimed to be the smartest guy in Ashland, but I'm not completely *stupid*."

"Pointing a gun at me is most definitely a stupid thing to do," Tucker said, his voice as cold as the wind gusting over the terrace.

Clyde laughed again. "Yeah, keep telling yourself that, tough guy. I saw how you looked at Lorelei the night we ran into her at Underwood's—like she was a big, juicy steak you wanted to sink your fangs into. And then what do I find tonight? The two of you sucking face in the bathroom like a couple of teenagers who can't keep their hands off each other."

I glanced at Tucker, but he was focused on Clyde, his face

as hard as I'd ever seen it. Another man, a smarter man, would have been very, very concerned about the barely restrained rage glinting in Tucker's eyes, but, like Clyde had said, he was far from the smartest man in Ashland.

"So as soon as I get my diamonds, you're also going to have a fatal accident, just like Lorelei is." Clyde jerked his head at Tucker. "Move. Now. Or I'll forgo the accident part altogether and shoot you where you stand. I need her to get into the shipping yard, not you."

Tucker's lips flattened out into a thin line, and that muscle twitched in his jaw again. He kept staring at Clyde, as though debating whether his vampiric speed would let him attack Clyde before the other man pulled the trigger. But Tucker must have realized that not even he was that fast, because he moved to the right.

Two of the giants stepped forward and clamped their hands around Tucker's arms, but he looked at me instead of them. His lips quirked up into a tiny grin, and I found myself smiling back at him. Hugh Tucker was a survivor, just like I was, and we were going to get through this—together.

Clyde turned away from the two giants, thinking they were capable of handling Tucker. Definitely not the smartest man in Ashland. This time, he jerked his head at me. "Come here. It's time to take that ride over to your shipping yard."

Just like Tucker, I did as commanded. Not because I was afraid of Clyde shooting me but because it got me—and especially him—closer to the icicles hanging off the edge of the resort roof.

"What else did Raymond tell you about me?" I asked.

Clyde's eyebrows drew together in thought. "Not much. Just that you were a whiny bitch who couldn't keep her mouth shut and was always crying to her mama about every little thing."

"Whiny bitch?" I nodded. "Yeah, that sounds about right. Raymond was never very creative. Not with his insults and especially not with his magic."

"What does that matter? Your brother is dead, and you're going to be joining him soon enough."

I grinned. "Oh, it matters quite a lot. Raymond might not have been terribly creative with his magic, but I am extremely creative with mine."

"Like I give a fuck about your magic," Clyde growled. "Now, come along quietly, or I'll shoot you in the kneecap, and you'll be too busy screaming to do anything else."

"Sure," I replied, holding my hands up. "Whatever you say."

Clyde eyed me, but he took a step back and glanced over at the third giant. "Go get the car—"

The second he looked away, I snapped up my hands even higher and blasted the resort roof with my Ice magic.

In an instant, loud, sharp, ominous noises zipped through the air.

Crack!

Crack! Crack!

Crack! Crack! Crack!

One after another, all those long, jagged icicles broke off the edge of the roof and dropped straight down onto Clyde's head, pelting him like a blizzard of icy nails. He yelped and staggered away, but I lunged after him.

Clyde cursed and lifted his gun to shoot me, but this time, I sent out a blast of metal magic, and his gun flew out of his hand, hit the terrace, and skittered away across the snow-covered flagstones.

He cursed again and chased after the weapon. I started to follow him, but a hand grabbed my arm, stopping me short. That same hand yanked me backward, and I bumped up against the chest of the third giant.

"You're not going anywhere!" he snarled.

Metal elementals weren't all that common. Even when people knew you had that kind of magic, they just never considered all the many, many ways you could use your power against them or just how much metal they constantly carried around, like on their clothes.

My gaze dropped to the silver pin shaped like an oversize dollar sign nestled in the center of the giant's tie. A grin spread across my face.

"What are you smiling at?" the giant growled.

Instead of answering him, I swiped out with my left hand, as though I was trying to claw his eyes out. The giant jerked his head back and dropped my other arm. The second I was free, I reached up and grabbed his tiepin with my right hand. With my elemental power, I didn't even have to rip it out of the silk, and the metal came to me quickly and easily, like a magnet *clacking* against my skin. A second wave of magic made the silver as pliable as putty, while a third wave of power changed the dollar sign, reshaping it into a small dagger with a razor-sharp point adorning the tip.

The giant growled and reached for me again. "What are you doing—"

I snapped my hand up and stabbed the reshaped tiepin straight into his left eye. The giant screamed, even as blood and other, more disgusting things spurted out of his face. I ripped the pin out of his eye and twirled it around in my fingers. Another wave of my magic reshaped the metal again, making the point even longer and sharper than before.

The giant staggered away, but I grabbed the end of his tie, yanked him back toward me, and buried the pin in the side of his neck. The giant screamed again, and even more blood spurted out of him than before, indicating that I'd hit something vital. Excellent.

My fingers were wet and slippery with the giant's blood, and

I couldn't pry the pin out of his neck, so I settled for shoving him away. He stumbled over one of the firepits and flopped down onto the terrace, his screams trailing off as his body shut down.

I whirled around to face another enemy. The two giants holding on to Tucker were staring at me, their mouths gaping in shock. They were so surprised by my killing their buddy that they weren't paying the slightest bit of attention to the vampire.

Last mistake they ever made.

Tucker casually shrugged off one giant's hand, not at all bothered by the other man's enormous strength and tight grip. Then he pivoted the other way, flinging off the second giant's hand as easily as he had the first. The smooth motions reminded me of a tiger stretching right before it killed its prey.

And Hugh Tucker was most definitely in a killing mood.

The first giant stumbled away, but the second man drew his fist back to punch the vampire. Despite the height difference between them, Tucker reached up, grabbed the giant's head, and snapped the other man's neck. He released the dead giant, who flopped down to the ground.

The first giant stared at Tucker, his mouth still gaping in shock, but some tiny part of his brain must have realized how much danger he was in, because he fumbled for the gun holstered to his belt. Tucker just stared at him, calmly watching while the other man grabbed the weapon and aimed it at him.

The moment reminded me of the vampire resolutely staring up at one of the stone balconies of the Mitchell mansion as it came crashing down toward him. Tucker would have just accepted his fate and let that rock crush him if I hadn't pulled him out of the way. Well, he might have a death wish, but I was prepared to save him again, even if it didn't seem like he wanted to be saved. I stepped forward and reached for my metal magic, ready to rip the gun out of the giant's hand—

A small smile curved Tucker's lips, and he finally moved.

The vampire morphed into a black blur moving almost too fast to follow. In an instant, Tucker had closed the distance between himself and the giant. In the next one, he'd ripped the gun out of the other man's hand and tossed it aside. The giant growled and took a swing at him, but Tucker ducked the blow, moving as smoothly and quickly as black ink spreading across a blank page.

He launched himself at the giant, and they both fell to the terrace. The giant snarled and flailed around with his fists, but Tucker dodged the frantic blows. He opened his mouth, and his fangs glinted an eerie, almost electric white in the golden light. Then Tucker snapped his head down and buried his fangs in the giant's throat.

The other man screamed and then screamed again as Tucker ripped his fangs out of the giant's neck. Blood sprayed everywhere, and the giant let out a sharp, keening wail that made goose bumps zip down my arms. He dropped back down to the ground, blood rapidly pooling under his body.

Tucker rolled off the giant, popped back up onto his feet, and faced me. Blood dripped down his chin and spattered onto his white shirt, but his black hair was still perfectly in place, and he wasn't even breathing hard. Annoying, frustrating, *and* deadly. A dangerously attractive combination. That hum in my body intensified, and I started to cross the terrace and make sure he was okay—

A hand grabbed my shoulder and spun me around. Before I could fight back, Clyde shoved his gun up against my stomach. I froze. Tucker growled and started forward, but Clyde shook his head in warning.

"Uh-uh. You stay right there, Hugh," he snarled. "Unless you want to watch your girlfriend bleed out."

Tucker stopped, but rage glinted in his eyes, and his hands

curled into fists, his knuckles as white as the snow covering the terrace.

Clyde stared down at the three giants we'd killed. "What a bloody mess. You two just *had* to make trouble, didn't you?"

"Says the man holding a gun on me," I snarked back.

"Shut up," he snapped.

Clyde spun me around and hooked his arm around my neck, using me as a human shield, even as he kept his gun pressed up against my side.

"You stay right there, Hugh," he warned. "And don't even *think* about trying to follow us, or I'll shoot Lorelei in the gut. That's a really painful way to die, and you don't want that, right?"

Tucker growled again, and the sound reverberated in my ears, joining that strange, delicious hum that was vibrating through the rest of my body.

"Don't worry about me," I called out. "I can take care of myself. I've been doing it for a long time now."

Tucker's gaze flicked to the giant I'd killed. "I never doubted you, Ms. Parker. I was just trying to do the gentlemanly thing and spare you from Clyde's less-than-honorable intentions."

"And they say that chivalry is dead," I drawled. "How very kind of you, Mr. Tucker."

Another one of those small smiles curved his lips, making him look even more handsome, despite the blood coating his mouth, chin, and neck.

"Shut up," Clyde snarled again, and started dragging me backward. "No one is interested in your not-so-witty banter."

Tucker's eyes narrowed in thought. He was clearly calculating whether he could kill Clyde before Clyde shot me. But I didn't need Hugh Tucker to rescue me. I was more than capable of saving myself.

Clyde kept dragging me backward, and I turned my head to the side so I could see where we were going. A few feet later, he had to stop and navigate around one of the firepits. He hesitated, then stepped to his left, moving over to the stone railing that lined the edge of the terrace. Perfect.

I reached out and ran my hand over the top of the railing, curling my fingers and gathering up the snow lying there. The chunks of snow weren't nearly as big, hard, and solid as the icicles I'd cracked off the roof earlier, but they would do the job. Just about anything would if you were creative enough with it.

And I was very, very creative with my magic.

Clyde wasn't an elemental, so he didn't sense my Ice power, and he didn't seem to notice my hand dragging through the snow or the cold crystals sticking to my fingers like glue. Tucker wasn't an elemental either, but his eyes narrowed a little more, and he tilted his head to the side, watching me. He knew I was up to something. He just didn't know what it was yet.

Clyde reached the stairs in the center of the terrace. He dropped his arm from around my neck and turned me around about halfway, so that I was standing more beside him than in front of him.

Clyde jabbed his gun into my side again, as if I needed a reminder that it was there. "We're going down the stairs. Don't try anything funny, or I'll shoot you right here and now and go get the diamonds myself."

"Oh, I wouldn't *dream* of trying anything funny," I drawled.

Suspicion filled his face, but I held up my right hand, as though I was meekly surrendering and giving in to all the awful things he wanted to do to me.

Tucker stepped forward, as though he was going to charge at Clyde after all.

The crime boss predictably looked in that direction. "I told you to stay put, you back-stabbing traitor—"

The second he glanced away from me, I brought up my left

hand, which was filled with snow, and smashed the icy wad of it into Clyde's face, right over his nose and mouth.

And then I glued it there.

I might not be the strongest elemental around, might not have half the magic that Gin Blanco and all the other powerhouses did, but you didn't have to be strong to kill someone with magic, just smart. And if there was one small, positive thing that had come out of dealing with my father and my brother, it was that they—and especially my mother—had made me smart and, perhaps more important, sneaky, determined, and ruthless.

So I shoved the snow as far up Clyde's nose as it would go and coated his mouth with what was left. Then I sent out another blast of magic. Instead of falling harmlessly away from his face, the snow stuck to his skin, the tiny flakes driven deep into his flesh by my cold, focused power.

Clyde made a choking sound, and he raised his free hand, trying to claw the snow off his nose and mouth. He managed to chip away a few chunks, ripping out his skin along with them, and blood welled up all around the snow, looking like a garish ring of red lipstick on his face.

Clyde kept clawing and clawing at the snow, desperately trying to tear it off so he could suck some air down into his lungs. He might have had a mix of giant and dwarven blood, might have been incredibly strong, but he still needed to breathe. Something he couldn't do right now, thanks to my little trick.

Desperation filled Clyde's eyes, but he still had enough wits left to point his gun at me again. I reached for my metal magic to wrench it out of his hand—

Quick as a blink, Tucker crossed the terrace, plucked the weapon out of Clyde's hand, and shoved the other man away from me. Clyde staggered back, still trying to claw the snow off his face. He tripped over one of the dead giants and lurched forward—right into the open space where the stairs were.

For a split second, Clyde hung in midair, like a diver launching himself off a platform over a swimming pool. Then he plummeted downward, and his head hit one of the steps with a sharp, audible *crack*. Gravity pulled him down several more steps before he finally came to rest on his back. Blood pooled under his head, but his eyes were already fixed and still, and he was obviously dead.

Side by side, Tucker and I stood there, staring down at Clyde's body.

"Neat trick," Tucker said, breaking the silence. "I've never seen an elemental kill someone with a snowball before."

"What can I say? I have many hidden talents."

"Yes, you do," he murmured. "Yes, you do."

He stared at me, and I looked right back at him. That hum in my body grew even louder and stronger than before, and I swayed toward him, despite the fact that we were both covered in blood and snow—

"What happened out here?" a familiar voice snapped in a peevish tone.

Tucker and I whirled around. Silvio was standing on the terrace, his hands planted on his hips. Liam was lurking behind him, surveying the bodies with a curious gaze.

"Well?" Silvio demanded. "What do you two have to say for yourselves?"

I shrugged. "You asked me if I had anything nefarious going on. Well, this is what *nefarious* looks like."

"I respectfully disagree," Tucker chimed in. "There's far too much blood and way too many bodies for this to be merely nefarious. *Slaughterous*, perhaps."

"*Slaughterous* isn't even a word," I replied.

He grinned. "Well, maybe it should be."

I grinned back at him.

"Well, *unbelievable* is most definitely a word, and it fits the two of you perfectly," Silvio said, his voice even more peevish than before. "I can't believe you two are flirting with each other at a time like this."

"What's the matter?" I asked. "You were the one who was saying how bored you were at the Pork Pit the other day. Why, the way you were talking, I would think you would welcome a little excitement."

Silvio threw his hands up into the air. "I don't mind dealing with dead bodies—during *normal* working hours. When your boss is an assassin, it's part of the job description. But this . . ." He gestured back and forth between himself and Liam. "This is *date night*. You don't leave blood and bodies strewn everywhere on date night!"

"Ah, now, don't be too hard on them," Liam said, slinging his arm around Silvio's shoulders. "Maybe Lorelei and Tucker just have a different definition of date night from ours."

Silvio sniffed and crossed his arms over his chest, as if he couldn't even fathom such a thing.

Me? Maybe I'd been hanging out with Gin too long, but I kind of liked this version of date night.

"Come on," Liam said, a wheedling note creeping into his voice. "Admit it. You live for this sort of stuff. It's part of what makes you such a terrific assistant—and such a great friend."

Silvio sniffed again, but he lowered his arms. "Fine. You're right. I'll admit that part of me is already thinking about the best way to get rid of these bodies." He brightened. "Let me text Sophia. I'm sure she has room in the trunk of her car for them. And then that way, I don't have to worry about messing up my van, especially since I just had it detailed."

Liam grinned. Silvio grinned back at him, then pulled his phone out of his jacket pocket.

"Thank you, Silvio," I said. "I owe you one."

He waved his hand at me, already lost in his device. "No worries, Lorelei. That's what friends are for."

Since Silvio and Liam had things under control, I turned to

Tucker. "I should get cleaned up and sneak back into the party before Mallory realizes what happened. I don't want to ruin her big night. Especially since she held the party specifically while Gin was gone in hopes that this sort of thing wouldn't happen."

Tucker held his arm out to me. "May I escort you back inside, Ms. Parker?"

I threaded my arm through his. "Why, that would be absolutely delightful, Mr. Tucker."

Together, the two of us strolled off the terrace, leaving the blood and bodies behind.

Yep, by Ashland standards, it was a perfect date night.

9

Tucker and I returned to the bathroom, which was still empty.

I washed the blood off my face, hands, and arms and made sure that none was visible on my dress. I also grabbed my purse from the floor, plucked out the comb and compact inside, and fixed my hair and makeup. Tucker scrubbed the blood off his mouth, but it wouldn't come out of his white shirt.

He dried his hands, tossed the paper towel into the trash, and faced me. "I should go finish cleaning up. And you should return to the party before Mallory misses you."

He was right. I should go, but I wanted some answers first.

"Why did you kill Walter Butler, the hit man Clyde sent after me?"

Tucker shifted on his feet, as though suddenly uncomfortable. "You know why."

"No, actually, I don't. Sometimes I think I know you so well. But other times, you are a complete and utter mystery."

"An annoying, frustrating, and stubborn mystery?" he asked in a teasing tone.

"Yes. All of those things and many others," I growled, tired of playing word games—and all the other games we seemed to be playing with each other. "Just tell me *why* you did it. And especially why you tried to hide the hit man's body afterward." He kept shifting on his feet, as though the motion would somehow make my question disappear. Finally, he sighed, stilled, and raised his eyes to mine.

"Because I like you far more than I have liked anyone in a long time," Tucker replied. "And I didn't want you to feel beholden to me, not for one instant, not for the smallest thing."

He sighed again, and weary resignation rippled through his long, slow exhale. "I know what it's like when someone does something for you and then expects something even greater in return. Not just expects it but *demands* it. When they put a hefty price tag on the help you so desperately need. And not a monetary price but something far more precious, little bits of your heart and soul and conscience and self-esteem that they take for themselves, one bloody favor at a time."

"Someone like Mason Mitchell?" I asked in a soft voice.

Tucker nodded, the jerk of his head as sharp as a silverstone knife slicing through the air. "Yes. After my father's gambling debts became too large and public to hide, Mason approached me. He was just starting his rise to power within the Circle, and he said he needed someone like me on his side, someone to help enact his vision for the group, a vision that would make us all richer and more powerful than we'd ever imagined. I was young and stupid at the time, and Mason was deceptively charismatic, so I foolishly believed him. I didn't see Mason for the monster he truly was until it was far too late, and he had already cost me much more than I had ever wanted to spend."

A haunted look filled his face, but I didn't ask what he was remembering—or what price he'd paid for Mason's greed and cruelty.

"The Circle had always dealt in various illegal enterprises in Ashland, and my father consorted with all sorts of unsavory people, gamblers, loan sharks, and the like. Anyone who would front him money, or play poker with him, or meet him for drinks at the casino or horse track that was his latest gambling obsession. So I didn't have a problem with Mason's vision for Ashland, not back then. Plus, it seemed like the only way to save my mother and the rest of my family from financial ruin."

"What happened?" I asked.

"Mason claimed that he would take care of all my father's debts, if only I would work for him."

"And you did."

Tucker nodded. "Mason was throwing me what seemed like a life preserver. I just didn't realize at the time that it was really an anchor."

His head dropped, his shoulders slumped, and his gaze fell to the tile floor, as if just thinking about all the awful things he'd done for Mason was another anchor dragging him down, down, down.

After several long, silent seconds, Tucker lifted his head and stared at me again. More of that weary resignation creased his face, and he looked utterly exhausted, far more exhausted than he had seemed even while he was recovering from almost dying at Mason's hands.

"I've done horrible things, Lorelei. Terrible, evil, unspeakable things. And I would have kept right on doing them if Gin hadn't learned about the Circle and killed Mason." Tucker's voice was low and raspy, but his words tolled out as loudly as a bell, as if marking each and every one of those dark, despicable, dirty deeds.

My heart ached for him, for everything he'd been through, for the awful position his father had put him in and the terrible things he'd had to do in order to survive. I opened my mouth to tell him that I understood, and especially that I didn't feel beholden to him, but Tucker gave me a sad, rueful smile.

"Mallory is probably wondering where you are. Good night, Ms. Parker."

Tucker tipped his head to me, then opened the door and stepped outside, leaving me alone in the bathroom with his confession still echoing in the air all around me.

I stared at the closed door for several seconds. Then I shook off my daze. What was I doing? I needed to go after Tucker and tell him . . . Well, I wasn't sure *what* I was going to tell him, but I had to try.

So I crossed the bathroom, opened the door, and stepped into the corridor, but of course, Tucker was long gone. I cursed the vampire's speed, but I headed to my right, away from the noise of the ballroom. Tucker wouldn't go there, which meant he was probably somewhere deeper in the resort—

"Pumpkin! There you are!" Mallory's voice boomed through the corridor. "Where have you been?"

I plastered a smile on my face, spun around, and walked over to her. "Sorry. It got a little hot and stuffy inside the ballroom, so I stepped outside to get some cool, fresh air."

Mallory arched an eyebrow. "Really? Is that why there are bloodstains all over your dress?"

I glanced down, but I didn't see any stains on the blue fabric, just a few damp spots from where I had already dabbed the blood away.

"What bloodstains?" I chirped in a bright voice.

Her eyebrow arched a little higher. "I'm more than three hundred years old, pumpkin. I can tell when you're lying. Plus, Silvio and Liam left the party several minutes ago, along with Sophia, and none of them has come back. You disappearing, along with the three of them, is a sure sign of trouble. So you might as well tell me what's going on."

I sighed, but I had never been able to sneak anything past my grandmother, so I filled her in on everything that had happened over the past few days, from Clyde O'Neal threatening me, to Tucker killing the hit man outside my mansion, to our fight with Clyde and his giants tonight.

"Silvio and Liam are outside dealing with the bodies, along with Sophia," I said, finishing my story.

Mallory crossed her arms over her chest. "Why didn't you tell me about any of this before now?"

"I didn't want to ruin your party."

She huffed. "Please. I was expecting something like this to happen. Why do you think I invited Silvio, Liam, and Sophia in the first place?"

I frowned. "Because they're our friends, and you wanted them to celebrate with you and Mosley?"

"Of course they're our friends, and I did want them to celebrate with Stuey and me. I love them all dearly."

"I hear a *but* in your voice."

Mallory grinned. "*But* they also happen to be very handy in certain situations. Besides, I learned an important lesson about planning parties a long time ago."

"What lesson?"

She shrugged. "That bad things are bound to happen in Ashland, *especially* at parties, so it's best to be prepared. And that nobody can handle bad things like us and our friends."

Laughter erupted out of my lips, loosening the knots of tension in my chest. I might be creative with my magic, but my grandmother was the smartest person I knew, which was one of the many reasons she was my hero.

"Well, now that you know what's going on, I should go help Silvio and the others."

A hopeful look filled Mallory's face. "Will Hugh Tucker be helping you too? Because a man like that could help with all *sorts* of things."

"Grandma!" I playfully swatted her shoulder. "In case you've forgotten, you are a married woman."

A blush spread across her cheeks, and a soft, dreamy look filled her blue eyes. "A very happily married woman." Her gaze sharpened. "But you, my dear, are quite single, and Hugh Tucker is quite handsome. Even better, he actually has a brain in that attractive noggin of his. And perhaps best of all, he looks at you the same way my Stuey looks at me."

"How is that?" I asked.

"Like he would do anything for you," Mallory replied. "Even hide out in the woods in the middle of a cold winter night to protect you from a killer and not take any credit for it after the fact."

She was right, but I still hesitated. "But what about everything he did for Mason and the rest of the Circle? Tucker might not have been at your wedding reception, but he still had a hand in ruining it. Just like he had a hand in kidnapping me, Gin, and Bria from the Posh boutique and in threatening me in the Circle cemetery outside the Mitchell mansion."

"Sure, Tucker has done a lot of bad things to us, but we've done some bad things to him in return." She gave me a chiding look. "You did stab him in the thigh with an Ice dagger and then basically hold him prisoner in a shipping container for a couple of weeks."

I grimaced at the reminders. "So?"

"So I'd say we're all more or less even. I can overlook those things for you, pumpkin. The question is, can you overlook and forgive him for them yourself?"

I thought of the raw pain and aching sadness in Tucker's voice when he'd told me about his father and the Circle and how he didn't want me to feel beholden to him the way he had been to Mason Mitchell. How we both constantly bottled up our feelings and put on a calm face for everyone around us. How we'd both been stuck in horrible situations and still survived them. But most of all, I thought of how my heart quickened and my entire body hummed whenever I was near him.

"I'm an idiot," I muttered.

Mallory nodded. "People often are when matters of the heart are involved."

"I should go find him." I glanced up and down the corridor again. "But he's probably already left the resort, and I have no idea where to look for him."

"Try room 1320."

I blinked. "What?"

"Room 1320, here at the resort," Mallory replied. "That's where Tucker is staying. He's been here ever since the night of the fight at the Mitchell mansion."

"How do you know that?"

Mallory shrugged again. "Finn and Silvio have their sources, and I have mine. Once Gin told me Tucker was staying in Ashland, I figured he would have to check into a hotel sooner or later. So I asked around, and a friend who works here at the resort was nice enough to email the information to me while Stuey and I were on our honeymoon."

"So you've known that Tucker was staying here this whole time?" Suspicion filled me. "Wait a second. Is that why you had your party here instead of at the country club again?"

A sly grin spread across her wrinkled face. "Well, you couldn't very well run into Tucker if we'd had the party at the country club."

Another laugh bubbled out of my lips. "I can't believe you set me up like this. You really *are* trying to play matchmaker."

Mallory's grin widened. "Something like that. I just want you to find the same sort of happiness that I've found, whether it's with Tucker or someone else."

She stepped forward and hugged me.

"I love you, Grandma," I rasped, emotion clogging my throat

as I returned her hug with an even tighter one of my own.

"Love you too, pumpkin."

We broke apart. Mallory cleared her throat and blinked back the tears gleaming in her eyes. Me too.

"I really should get back to the party. Stuey and the guests will be wondering where I am. And I believe you have a date to rustle up." She gave me a saucy wink. "I'll call you in the morning, and you can give me *all* the juicy details."

"Is that so?" I asked, a smile spreading across my face.

"Absolutely." Mallory patted my arm, then headed back toward the ballroom.

I waited until she had vanished around the corner, then strode in the opposite direction. A minute later, I reached a bank of elevators and stepped inside one. The door slid shut, but the car didn't move. I stared at the panel, my index finger hovering over the button marked *13*.

Doubt crept over me. About myself, my feelings for Tucker, and especially his for me. But everyone else was moving on with their lives, and it was time for me to do the same. And right now, I wanted Hugh Tucker. I'd worry about everything else later.

I punched the button, and the elevator started to rise.

10

I got off on the appropriate floor and made my way to room 1320, which was located at the end of the corridor. Before I lost my nerve, I raised my hand and knocked on the door. A few seconds later, it opened, and Tucker appeared.

He'd shed his ruined tuxedo jacket, bow tie, and cummerbund, although he was still wearing his white shirt and black pants. His shirt was unbuttoned, and his feet were bare, which somehow made him even more ridiculously attractive.

Surprise filled his face. "Lorelei? What are you doing here?"

Instead of answering, I stepped past him and found myself in a luxury suite, complete with a kitchen and a sitting area filled with chairs and a long couch arranged in front of a fireplace. A door off to the right led into the bedroom, along with an attached bathroom.

I tossed my purse down onto the kitchen counter, then faced him. "I came here to tell you that you're wrong."

"About what?"

"Pretty much everything."

I stepped out of my kitten heels and used my foot to scoot them off to the side.

He frowned. "What are you doing?"

I gestured at his bare feet. "Just leveling the playing field."

His frown deepened, but he kept staring at me. "Okay. So what, exactly, am I wrong about?"

"For starters, the notion that I might feel beholden to you for saving me from that hit man." I reached around and tugged down the zipper on the back of my dress. "I wanted to make it crystal-clear right from the start that I feel no such beholdenment."

"That's not a word," he protested.

"It is now."

I drew the dress down off my arms, stepped out of it, and scooped it up off the floor. Then I folded the garment and set it on the kitchen counter next to my purse. The air was a bit cool, and I shivered in my blue bra and matching undies. Tucker's gaze trailed over my body, and suddenly, I wasn't cold at all.

"As for you doing bad things, well, I've probably done just as many, including killing my own brother. It doesn't get much darker and more vicious than that. So I would say we are evenly matched in that regard."

He didn't respond, but his gaze remained locked on my body, and his hands clenched into fists, as though he was fighting the urge to reach for me.

"Something else you should know is that I like to be prepared." I opened my purse and drew out a condom. I showed it to him, then set it down on the counter. "I also take birth control pills."

He still didn't respond, but his fists clenched a little tighter, his knuckles standing out like white stars against his tan skin.

"Now, I could be wrong, but it seems like we've spent the past several weeks doing this weird sort of flirting and tiptoeing around our mutual attraction. Well, I don't want to tiptoe around anything anymore. So I came here to tell you what

I want, what I've wanted for a long time now—and that is *you*, Mr. Tucker."

"This is a bad idea," he rasped, although his gaze never left my body.

I strolled forward, swinging my hips just a bit, and stopped right in front of him. "See? There you go again, being wrong about everything. Because I happen to think it's an *excellent* idea."

He kept staring at me. When it was clear he wasn't going to make the first move, I reached up, pushed the flaps of his shirt aside, and smoothed my hands down his bare chest. He sucked in a ragged breath, and his muscles bunched and flexed under my light, teasing touch.

"So warm and firm," I murmured.

He still didn't move, so I stepped forward and buried my face in the crook of his neck. His cologne washed over me, and the spicy scent made my head spin. Mmm.

I drew back and looked up at him. Hunger filled his face, and the raw, naked emotion made me shiver again, this time in anticipation.

Tucker loosened his fists, then slowly reached up and cupped my cheek. He trailed his fingertips down my face and throat, stopping at the pulse that was hammering in my neck.

"I can hear your heart," he rasped again, a note of wonder in his voice. "Beating hard and fast, just like mine is."

He grabbed my hand and placed it on his own heart as if to confirm his words. I flattened my palm against his chest, drinking in the delicious warmth of his skin against mine. Then I curled my other hand around his neck and drew his mouth down to mine.

All my previous restraint vanished the instant our lips touched. I plunged my tongue into Tucker's mouth, and he growled low in his throat and kissed me back just as fiercely. Suddenly, I couldn't kiss him quick enough, couldn't touch him long enough, couldn't feel enough of him pressing up against me. I tugged impatiently on the sides of his shirt, trying to shove it out of the way. Tucker drew back and ripped it off, then stepped into my arms again.

We spun around and around, lips and tongues clashing together time and time again, even as our hands roamed all over each other's body. Somehow I ended up with my back against the door. Tucker stood before me, his gaze raking over me again.

"You're so beautiful," he murmured in a low, reverent voice. "Inside and out. Far too beautiful for me."

His compliment warmed me from head to toe, inside and out, and I crooked my finger at him. "Then come here and show me exactly how beautiful you think I am."

A devilish grin spread across his face, and he stepped forward.

Tucker kissed me again, his hands gliding up my back, and I moved away from the door so that he could unhook my bra. I slid it down my arms and tossed it aside. Tucker's hands landed on my breasts, and he rolled one nipple in his fingers, while he bent down and sucked on the other one.

I moaned and arched back. Every gentle tweak and hard suck sent a fresh wave of desire spiking through my body, and a wet heat pooled between my thighs. I reached down and stroked his thick, hard erection through his pants, wanting to bring him the same sort of pleasure he was giving me. Tucker hissed out a breath and drew back, his black eyes glimmering with desire.

I stroked him a few seconds longer, then opened his pants and slid my hand inside. My fingers closed around his erection, and he hissed again, his lips drawing back and his fangs flashing like pointed white pearls in his mouth.

"I've dreamed about you touching me like this," he said in a low, strained voice. "And touching you in return."

"Really?" I drawled, still stroking him. "What did you have in mind?"

Tucker's hands settled on my waist. He tugged on the edges of my panties, and I moved away from the door so that he could drop to his knees and slide them down my legs. I stepped out of the panties and kicked them aside. Still on his knees, Tucker grinned, leaned forward, and put his mouth on me.

He fell into the same rhythm he'd lavished on my breasts, gentle tweaks and long, hard sucks that made one wave of pleasure after another crash over me. I fell back against the door, squirming, trembling, and moaning even louder than before, but it wasn't enough. I wanted more—more of *him*.

So I grabbed his shoulders and tugged him back up my body. He came willingly, and this time, I went to work on his pants, sliding them down, along with his black boxers. I stroked him again, and he trembled against me the same way I had trembled against him.

Tucker backed me up against the door again and caught my mouth in another deep, hungry kiss. I ran my fingers through his hair, finally mussing the silky locks the way I had wanted to for weeks now. Tucker rained kisses down my neck, stopping to tease my throat with his teeth.

"Bite me," I rasped.

His lips froze on my neck, and he slowly drew back and looked at me.

"In the shipping container, you told me how good that could be, if both parties are willing," I said, answering the silent question in his eyes. "So bite me."

"Are you sure?" he asked in a soft voice.

"Yes. Bite me." I paused. "Please."

His eyes glowed like black stars, and a wicked grin spread across his face. "Well, since you said please . . ."

His lips drew back, revealing his fangs again, and he leaned forward, his gaze focused on my neck. My fingers dug into his shoulders, and my breath hitched in anticipation.

I wasn't sure what I was expecting, but his fangs slid into my skin with the faintest, smallest sting of pain. A shudder rippled through him, and that hum in my own body grew a little louder. Tucker drew in a long, slow, deep breath, then sucked on my neck, using his lips on my skin and his fangs deeper inside me.

That small sting of pain vanished, replaced by a pulse of pure desire that rocketed through my entire body. Tucker sucked on my neck again. It was a small, soft, gentle motion, as though he was taking a sip of a fine wine and wanted to savor every single drop, but I felt the sensation all the way down into my bones. A sharp, pounding ache erupted between my legs, and I squirmed around, trying to get even closer to him, trying to feel every last inch of him pressing into me the same way his fangs were.

"You taste like snow and steel," Tucker murmured against my skin. "Delicious."

"More. Now. Please." I rasped out the words, my desire for him so intense that I didn't want to waste time trying to form a coherent sentence.

Tucker drew back, plucked the condom off the counter, and covered himself with it. Then he grabbed my hips and lifted me up. I locked my legs around his waist. He stared at me, another silent question in his eyes. I nodded, and he moved forward, pressing my back against the door.

We kissed, our tongues dancing and dueling together. Then Tucker's lips slid down my neck, and his fangs sank into my skin again. Another small sting shot through me, but this one was far more pleasure than pain, and I shuddered at the sensation.

Tucker drew in another breath, as though steadying himself, then sucked on my neck and thrust deep inside me at the same time. I gasped at how good it felt.

"More. Now. Please." Once again, I didn't bother with a complete sentence.

Tucker surged forward again and again and again, matching the rhythm of his thrusts to every drop of blood he pulled out of my neck. I dug my hands into his back, yanking him closer and urging him on at the same time.

Stings of pain, spikes of pleasure. It was all one and the same, with our hearts beating as hard and fast as our bodies were rocking together.

It was everything I'd ever dreamed it would be and more—so much *more*.

Tucker thrust into me again and groaned, finding his release. As his body bucked against mine, he took a long, slow drag on my neck, and an orgasm ripped through me as well. Fire exploded in my body, bringing with it a sweet, intense rush of feeling, like a thousand little heart stings hitting me all at once.

✿ 11 ✿

I wasn't sure how much time passed before the amazing, intense high faded, and I slowly came back to myself.

Tucker removed his fangs from my neck. He kissed the spot where he had bitten me, then lifted his head. His black eyes blazed with the same warmth I felt in my own heart. He withdrew from my body, but instead of letting me down, he carried me into the other room and gently placed me on the bed. I collapsed back against the pillows, too satisfied and sated to do anything else right now.

Tucker went into the bathroom, disposed of the condom, and washed his hands. A few seconds later, he returned carrying a glass of water.

"Here. Drink this. You need to stay hydrated."

I took the water and started sipping it. Tucker lay down next to me and drew a blanket up over our bodies. I finished the water and set the glass on the nightstand. Then I lay down next to him, resting my hand on his chest.

Thump-thump-thump.

His heart was still beating hard and fast, and the rhythm reminded me of our bodies coming together time and time again.

"Did that live up to your expectations, Ms. Parker?" Tucker asked, a teasing note in his voice.

"And then some, Mr. Tucker. How was it for you?"

"Exceptional. Phenomenal. Sensational."

I grinned, scooted forward, and kissed him again. We broke apart, and his eyes glittered with fresh heat.

His hand crept around to my back, and he started drawing circles on my skin. Each light skim of his fingertips made a delicious shiver sweep through me.

"You got your fantasy about me biting you," Tucker murmured, even more heat sparking in his eyes. "Well, I have some fantasies of my own when it comes to you."

"Really?" I purred. "Well, why don't you start from the top, and we'll work our way down your list?"

"With pleasure," he murmured, and lowered his lips to mine again.

We spent the rest of the night exploring our various fantasies, some of which were mutual and all of which were quite enjoyable.

Early the next morning, I woke up nestled in Tucker's arms. For a long time, I just lay there, watching the sunlight and shadows sweep across his face and body, which were both soft and relaxed with sleep. The longer I lay there, the more a hard truth settled in my heart.

Somehow, despite all the danger and dark deeds that had transpired between us, I had fallen for Hugh Tucker, and I had no idea what to do about my feelings for him.

"I didn't realize you enjoyed watching other people sleep," he murmured, cracking his eyes open. "It's a bit creepy."

"Just you," I replied, startled by the honesty in my voice. "You are a very watchable person, even while asleep. I never know what you're going to do next."

"I could say the same thing about you."

I scooted a little closer, and his arm curled around me. We stayed in bed, dozing and drinking in each other's presence . . . until a loud chirp emanated from the kitchen.

Tucker's eyes snapped open. "Is that an alarm?"

I groaned and sat up. "Yes, my alarm. Unfortunately, I have some interviews this morning."

"Interviews? For what?"

I wrapped a blanket around my body and stood up. "An open position in my company. The last person who had the job betrayed me, and I killed him for it. I've been looking for a replacement ever since."

Tucker stared at me, his face unreadable.

"Sorry. I know it's not the usual morning-after pillow talk."

He arched an eyebrow. "There is nothing usual about you, Lorelei Parker, which is one of the many things I like about you."

I grinned, then went into the bathroom and shut the door behind me. I studied my reflection in the mirror. Mussed black hair, bright blue eyes, flushed skin. I looked like someone who was still feeling the afterglow from last night. My gaze dropped to my neck. Two red punctures marred my skin, but they were much smaller than I'd expected. The marks certainly didn't capture the scope of all the things I'd done with Tucker, and they especially didn't convey the enormity of all the things I felt for him now.

But I ignored the heart stings reverberating through my chest, locked my feelings down tight, and plastered a smile on my face as I stepped back out into the bedroom where Tucker was waiting.

We both got dressed, me in last night's dress and him in a fresh suit, and met in the kitchen. He poured me a glass of orange juice, which I gulped down while I checked my phone.

Most of my messages were from Karlotta, reminding me about the interviews and cheerfully threatening to quit herself if I didn't show up as promised. I sighed. As much as I wanted to stay here in this happy bubble, the real world was waiting, and it was time to return to my regularly scheduled life. Now that Clyde O'Neal was no longer a threat, maybe I would have an easier time picking—and trusting—whomever I hired as my number two. Probably not, given my lack of progress on the matter so far, but I had to try.

I drained the last of my juice, set my glass aside, and faced Tucker, who was leaning up against the kitchen counter.

"Time for the awkward goodbye talk?" he asked in a soft voice.

"Only if you don't want to see me again."

He blinked in surprise, as if he hadn't expected me to say such a thing. I'd surprised myself too, but I wasn't going to take back my words. I did want to see Tucker again, and not just for a repeat performance of everything we'd done last night. I actually *liked* the vampire. He was smart and witty and had a dry sense of humor that matched my own.

"You wish to continue our . . . association?" he asked.

"Don't you?" I countered. "Because it seemed like we both had a pretty good time *associating* with each other last night."

"More than just *pretty good*, Ms. Parker. Don't sell yourself short. Why, I would go so far as to use words like *superb* and *stupendous* to describe our associating."

Pleasure hummed through me at the compliments. "Aw, Mr. Tucker, you flatter me."

"I do try, Ms. Parker."

He grinned at me, and some of the awkwardness between us faded. My phone let out another warning chirp.

"But for right now, I really do have to go." I hesitated. "Can I . . . call you later?"

He nodded. "I would like that very much."

I hesitated again, then kissed his cheek and left the suite. The soft *click* of the door shutting behind me boomed as loudly as a crack of thunder in the quiet corridor.

I stood there, staring at the smooth wood, wondering if we would actually keep the promises we'd just made to each other or if this was really an ending rather than a beginning.

I shook off my doubt and melancholy, left the resort, and went home. By the time I took a shower, changed clothes, and drove over to the shipping yard, it was almost noon and time for my first interview of the day.

Karlotta Valdez was sitting at her desk, typing on a keyboard, when I stepped into the office. She was a lovely woman, in her fifties, with short, curly black hair, ebony skin, and brown eyes. Red glasses perched on the end of her nose, the color a perfect match to her stylish pantsuit and glossy lipstick.

Karlotta pointedly looked up at the clock on the wall, then back over at me. "You're cutting it close. The first interview is supposed to be here in less than fifteen minutes."

"I know, I know, I'm running late." I placed a cup on the end of her desk, along with a large box. "But I did bring you a peppermint mocha from the Cake Walk, along with a box of those raspberry cream-cheese Danishes you like so much."

Karlotta sniffed. "As if I can be bought off with a coffee and some pastries."

"Well, if you don't want them . . ."

She scooted both the coffee and the box out of my reach. "I didn't say that."

Karlotta cracked open the box, grabbed a Danish, and sank her teeth into the pastry. "Mmm. Scratch that. I can definitely be bought off with a coffee and some pastries."

She saluted me with the Danish. I grinned and headed into

my office. My gaze landed on the fresh pile of manila folders on my desk. I sighed and trudged forward. I needed to review the résumés before folks started arriving for their interviews—

Crack!

Once again, I slammed my knee into the side of that stupid filing cabinet. Pain spiked through my leg, and curses spewed out of my mouth. I drew my leg back to kick the offending metal when I noticed just how far out of line the cabinet was with all the others.

Almost like something was wedged in between it and the wall.

Dimitri Barkov and his crew robbed a fancy jewelry store . . . millions in diamonds . . . Dimitri bragged to me that he still had the stones hidden in his office. Clyde O'Neal's voice whispered through my mind.

Given everything that had happened with Tucker last night, I'd forgotten what Clyde had revealed about why he'd wanted my shipping yard so badly and the treasure that might still be in here, just waiting for me to find it.

Pain forgotten, I grabbed my phone out of my purse and turned on the flashlight app. Then I crouched down and shone the light behind the filing cabinet. Surely, Dimitri Barkov had picked a better, more discreet and creative hiding place than this . . .

Nope. Dimitri hadn't been the smartest man in Ashland either. The light landed on a black leather briefcase that was wedged in between the cabinet and the wall. Excitement surged through me. It took me several hard, determined yanks, but I finally pried the briefcase out of its hidey-hole. The motion made me stagger backward, and this time, I rammed my other knee into the side of the desk. Another string of curses spewed out of my mouth.

"Lorelei?" Karlotta's voice drifted through my closed office door. "Are you okay?"

"Fine!" I yelled. "Just moving some furniture around."

"Okay," Karlotta said, although doubt filled her voice. "Let me know if you need any help."

"Will do!"

I waited a few seconds to make sure she wasn't going to poke her head inside the office, then slung the briefcase down onto my desk. To my surprise, it wasn't even locked, so I flipped up the metal flaps and slowly cracked the lid open to reveal . . .

Diamonds—*lots* of diamonds.

The briefcase was lined with black velvet compartments fitted with tiny clear plastic doors, and each section was filled with diamonds. White, pink, blue, black. The colors were dazzling, as was the way the stones caught and reflected the light.

I let out a low, appreciative whistle. "Hello, gorgeous girls."

I wasn't an expert like Mallory, but even I could tell that I was looking at several million dollars in diamonds. No wonder Clyde had been so desperate to get his hands on my shipping yard. A score like this would have solved all his rumored money problems.

A bit dazed by my discovery, I plopped down into my chair. My mind started whirring, wondering what to do next. I couldn't keep the diamonds in my office. Sure, Clyde O'Neal was dead, but someone in his organization might know that the gemstones were here and come after them—and me.

I rocked back in my chair and weighed my options. I could take the diamonds to First Trust bank. Mosley would be happy to put them in a safety-deposit box until I figured out what to do with them, and Finnegan Lane would be more than willing to help me turn the stones into cash that I could add to my bank accounts. But I hadn't stolen the diamonds myself, so it didn't feel right to just keep them. I might be a criminal, but I still earned my money, just like everyone else did—

An idea popped into my mind. Suddenly, I knew *exactly*

what to do with the diamonds. I shut the briefcase and hit a button on my phone.

"Hey, Lorelei," Karlotta's voice flooded my office. "Do you need something?"

"Please get a messenger over here. I have a package that needs to be delivered."

✱ 12 ✱

Karlotta helped me box up the briefcase. She didn't ask what was inside it, although she did do a double take when I revealed whom I wanted it sent to.

Karlotta frowned. "Are you sure?"

A grin spread across my face. "Absolutely."

She gave me another confused look, but she summoned the messenger, and we shipped out the box.

I spent the rest of the afternoon interviewing one person after another. Several of the folks were capable, all were supremely confident, and a few were already plotting against me. But none of them was quite right, so I sent them all on their way with empty promises to call as soon as I'd made a decision.

By the time four o'clock rolled around, I was sick of padded résumés, rehearsed answers, and fake smiles. I set the last folder on the discard pile with all the others and resisted the urge to sweep them all off my desk and into the trash can waiting below. It truly was so hard to find good help, especially good criminal help.

I sighed and cracked my neck from side to side, trying to

relieve some of the tension that had gathered in my body.

Karlotta knocked on the open door and stepped into my office. "Hey, Lorelei. I've got one more person for you to see."

I gestured at the stack of folders. "But I thought that last woman was the final interview of the day."

"We have a surprise applicant," she replied, a strange note in her voice. "They just . . . showed up and asked about the job, so I thought I would see if you felt like doing one more interview."

I bit back a groan, but I might as well get it over with. "Sure. Send them in."

Karlotta nodded and moved away from the door. She murmured something, and then the faint scuff of footsteps sounded, heading in this direction. I stood up and plastered a polite smile on my face, trying to ignore the ache in my cheeks—

Hugh Tucker stepped into my office.

His visit wasn't entirely unexpected, but the sight of him still made my heart race. "What are you doing here?"

"I got your message." He strode over and placed a familiar black leather briefcase on top of my desk. "I have to admit that I was quite surprised by the contents. No one has ever sent me millions of dollars in diamonds before."

"What can I say? I'm original that way."

A grin spread across his lips. "Yes, you are."

He gestured at the briefcase. "I take it you found the diamonds that Dimitri Barkov stole."

I pointed over at the filing cabinet, which was still out of line with all the others. "Right over there."

He nodded. "But why did you send them to me? Why not keep them for yourself?"

"Because I didn't earn them. You did. You were the one who pretended to work for Clyde O'Neal and took out the hit man he sent after me and then helped me kill him and his men last night. So if anyone deserves those diamonds, it's you."

A frown creased his face. "I didn't do any of that for a briefcase full of diamonds. I didn't even know about the diamonds until Clyde mentioned them at the resort last night. I just thought he wanted your shipping yard so he could expand his own business."

Tucker's words loosened an enormous knot of worry in my chest. He truly hadn't known about the diamonds, which meant that everything we'd shared last night had been completely genuine. I hadn't realized how important that distinction was to me until this very moment, but I still needed more answers.

"If you didn't know about the diamonds, then why did you do all those things?"

"For you," he replied. "I did them all for you, Lorelei."

His soft words sent another heart sting shooting through my chest. Despite my best effort to play it cool, I couldn't stop a pleased grin from spreading across my face. "That's one of the loveliest things anyone has ever said to me."

"You should have someone in your life who says lovely things to you every single day," Tucker replied.

"Are you volunteering for the job?"

"Perhaps." He straightened up to his full height. "If we can come to acceptable terms."

Confusion filled me. "Terms about what?"

Tucker nudged the briefcase aside, then reached into his suit jacket, pulled out a folded piece of paper, and handed it to me. I opened the sheet and scanned the contents.

My gaze snapped up to his. "This is a résumé."

He nodded, squared his shoulders, and smoothed his hand down his tie. "Yes, it is. One typically brings a résumé to a job interview."

My eyebrows shot up in surprise. "You're here to apply for a job? I thought that was just a line you used to get past Karlotta."

"Yes, since Gin killed Mason, I find myself without lawful employment." He paused. "Well, more like unlawful employment, given my previous work history."

My eyes narrowed. "And you want to work for me? Why?"

"Well, you could obviously use my skills and expertise in your organization." A sly grin spread across his face. "And I happen to like you far better than any of the other underworld bosses."

I snorted, but his comment did make me grin in return. Still, my mood quickly turned serious again. "You don't owe me anything. That's why I sent you the diamonds. So that neither one of us would be beholden to the other."

"On the contrary, I owe you everything," he replied. "And I want to work for you much like Silvio Sanchez works for Gin."

I frowned again. "What do you mean?"

Tucker held his hands out to his sides. "I don't know how to do or be anything other than a bad guy, and I have no desire to start my own criminal empire. There's far too much paperwork involved. So if I'm going to work for an underworld boss, then it should be someone I respect and admire, among other things."

My heart squeezed tight. "What other things?"

Tucker's black eyes gleamed in his face. "It's quite a long list, much longer and far more detailed than we have time for in this interview, so let me sum it up. I care about you, Lorelei, and I want to do everything in my power to ensure your continued health and happiness."

More warmth filled me at his words, but I forced myself to ask the obvious questions. "How would this work? Given that you know me far better than you do any other underworld boss?"

Tucker shrugged yet again. "Business is business. Here you're the boss. I will offer advice when asked, but I will always defer to your decisions."

"And after business hours?" I asked, a husky note creeping into my voice.

Heat sparked in his eyes. "Oh, I think we can mutually defer to each other after business hours."

An answering grin spread across my face. "Well, then, consider yourself hired, Mr. Tucker."

"Thank you, Ms. Parker," he purred. "I believe this is just the beginning of our mutually beneficial relationship."

He held out his hand, and we shook on it, sealing this new bargain between us.

Since Tucker was here, and it was still technically business hours, I introduced him to Karlotta, then took him outside and introduced him to Dario as well. The two men shook hands, although the giant eyed the vampire with open suspicion. Still, they were both honorable in their own ways, and I thought they would get along well, once some of their mutual distrust faded.

I also gave Tucker a tour of the warehouse, along with the actual shipping yard, and showed him how everything worked. He listened to and absorbed everything I said and asked several smart questions in return. My feelings for him aside, I could already tell that Tucker would be a big asset to my organization.

Our tour ended at the back of the shipping yard, at the container where he had spent all those weeks recovering.

Tucker gestured at the door. "May I?"

"Sure."

He opened it, and we both stepped inside. He waited for me to turn on the lights, then studied the space with a critical eye.

"I love what you've done with the place," he drawled.

I laughed. "Thanks."

Tucker went over and sat down on the cot. Then he looked up at me. "I wanted to see if the view had changed."

"What view?"

"Of you."

I frowned. "What do you mean?"

He gestured around the container. "I was in terrible shape after the cemetery fight with Mason. Not just my body but my mind and heart too. But being here with you, having you challenge and push me at every single turn, was the best thing that could have happened to me. Because you made me wake up and want to fight—you made me want to actually *live* again instead of just going through the motions."

His gaze locked with mine. "But mostly, this will always be a special spot because it's where I started falling in love with you, Lorelei."

My body froze, even as my heart leaped forward like a race car speeding around a track. His head tilted to the side, as though he could hear how hard and fast it was beating.

Tucker cleared his throat and stood up. "I don't expect you to return the sentiment. I just wanted you to know how I feel."

He started to step outside, but I moved forward, blocking his path.

"I also have a surprising fondness for this metal box," I replied in a soft voice. "Because this is where I started falling in love with you too, Hugh."

A smile spread over his face, and he held out his hand. I threaded my fingers through his and gave them a firm squeeze.

Tucker's smile slid off his face, replaced by a familiar hungry look. "You know, we didn't get to all of my fantasies last night," he said in a low, husky voice. "Over the past few weeks, I've had some rather interesting thoughts about that cot over there."

"Really?" I purred. "How fascinating. Because my fantasies mostly involved you and that table."

He glanced down at his watch. "It's after five, which means it is officially after business hours—and time for us to defer to each other, Ms. Parker. If you so wish, of course."

I returned his wicked grin with one of my own. "I think that's an excellent idea, Mr. Tucker. Just let me make sure that we won't be disturbed."

I pulled on the handle, and the door slowly started to close. Tucker stepped forward and lowered his mouth to mine. I wound my fingers through his perfect hair, mussing it up and getting ready to do the same thing to him, again and again.

I drew him deeper into the shipping container, and the door banged shut behind us just like the hotel door had closed behind me this morning. But now I knew the sound for what it truly was: the start of a new chapter for the two of us—together.

WINTER'S

An Elemental Assassin Novella

JENNIFER ESTEP

*To all the fans of the Elemental Assassin series
who wanted more stories—this one is for you.*

*To all the fans—never stop enjoying
the things that make you happy.*

Author's Note

Winter's Web takes place after the events of **Venom in the Veins**, book 17 in the **Elemental Assassin** urban fantasy series.

Winter's Web first appeared in the **Seasons of Sorcery** anthology in 2018.

* 1 *

"I look *ridiculous*."

I stared at my reflection in the mirror above the long counter that ran along the wall. Even though I had been peering at myself for the better part of a minute, I still couldn't believe what I was seeing.

Normally, my wardrobe could best be described as *functional*. Black boots, dark jeans, a long-sleeved T-shirt, a fleece jacket if the weather was cold. I never invested a lot of time or money in my clothes, since they had an annoying tendency to get ripped, torn, and covered with other people's blood.

But today I had left functional behind for *flamboyant*.

A royal-blue silk blouse with ruffles running down the front stretched across my chest. As if the color wasn't bright and bold enough, the entire garment was also covered with shiny thread, glittering sequins, and tiny feathers, all in black. I looked like I'd killed a couple of crows and was proudly wearing their fluttering feathers as some sort of macabre trophy. Plus, the sequins caught the light with every breath I took, and they winked at me in the mirror like dozens of little evil eyes.

But that was only the beginning of my unfortunate ensemble.

In addition to the dead-bird blouse, I was also wearing a black leather lace-up corset covered with even more black feathers and sequins. The tight corset pushed my breasts up to new and impressive heights, and my sudden abundance of cleavage was on display for all to see, thanks to the blouse's deep scooped neckline.

The plunging neckline also showed off the silverstone pendant resting in the hollow of my throat—a small circle surrounded by eight thin rays. A spider rune, my rune, and the symbol for patience. A matching ring stamped with my spider rune gleamed on my right index finger, and the same symbol was branded into each of my palms.

Tight black leather pants and knee-high black leather boots, both trimmed with royal-blue thread and even more black sequins and feathers, completed my outrageous outfit.

Normally, royal blue was one of my favorite colors, but this outfit screamed *Look at me!* in all the wrong ways. The only good thing about the atrocious ensemble was that the abundance of thread, sequins, feathers, and flounces hid the two silverstone knives I had up my sleeves. Another knife was tucked in the small of my back underneath the horrible corset, and two more rested in the sides of my boots.

"Well, I think you look great," a bright voice chirped, interrupting my dark musings. "Really in the spirit of the season."

A man stepped up beside me and checked his own reflection in the mirror. His long-sleeved shirt and pants were both made of bright green velvet trimmed with even brighter purple silk stripes, making him look like an oddly flavored candy cane. A matching green-and-purple-striped velvet hat with three long, pointed, floppy ends topped his head, while the toes of his green velvet slippers curled up to form soft purple triangles.

Finnegan Lane, my foster brother, reached up and carefully adjusted one of the shiny silver bells on the end of his hat. All that velvet made his eyes seem greener than usual, although the ridiculous hat hid most of his walnut-brown hair.

"What are you supposed to be again?" I asked.

Finn lifted his chin with pride. "*I* am a court jester, ready to entertain the masses with my charming wit, amazing skills, and dashing good looks."

"Really? Because I think all that green velvet makes you look like one of Santa's elves who couldn't find his way back to the North Pole."

Finn glared at me, but the other people in the room snickered at my joke.

"Forget about you." I held my arms out wide. "I don't even know what character I'm supposed to be."

Finn grinned and opened his mouth, but I stabbed my finger at him in warning.

"If you say *serving wench*, then I am going to make you eat that jester's hat, velvet, bells, and all," I growled.

He cleared his throat, changing course. "Well, I was going to say *pirate queen*, but why don't we just go with *assassin*? After all, that is your usual nighttime occupation."

I made a face, but he was right. During the day, to most normal people, I was Gin Blanco, owner of the Pork Pit barbecue restaurant in downtown Ashland. But at night, to the shady folks on the wrong side of the law, I was the Spider, a deadly assassin and the supposed queen of the city's underworld.

"Well, pirate queen, assassin, or whatever else you want to call me, I still look ridiculous," I grumbled. "Fletcher would roll over in his grave if he saw me dressed like this."

Fletcher Lane had been Finn's dad and my assassin mentor. And just like me, Fletcher had always been far more comfortable in his old blue work clothes than anything else.

"Nah," Finn said. "He'd laugh his ass off, then make us pose for pictures."

He was right again. The two of us shared a smile at the thought of the old man, and then my brother shook his head.

"Don't blame me for this," Finn said. "This was all Owen's idea."

"Oh, trust me, I haven't forgotten that."

I turned to look at the other man in the room. He too was dressed in costume, although his was far more subdued: a black silk shirt under a dark gray leather vest, along with matching gray leather pants and black boots. Like Finn, he was also wearing a hat, but his was much simpler, a black leather cap with two long flaps that covered his ears, along with most of his black hair.

Despite the costume, the sight of his strong, muscled body and handsome features, including his slightly crooked nose and the scar that cut across his chin, made my heart skip a beat, especially when he fixed his violet gaze on my gray one.

"I don't know what you're talking about," Owen Grayson, my significant other, rumbled. "I am but a humble blacksmith today, remember?"

I huffed and crossed my arms over my chest. Instead of being intimidated by my continued grumbling, Owen stepped forward, grabbed my hand, and dropped to one knee in front of me.

He grinned. "Although this humble blacksmith is always happy to serve his lady, the Spider, a fearsome pirate queen assassin and the purveyor of the finest barbecue in all the realms."

I huffed again at his cheesy words and theatrics, but I couldn't help but grin back at him. "You are getting way more into this than I expected."

Owen flashed me another grin, then climbed to his feet. He was still holding my hand, and the warmth of his skin soaked into mine. "Oh, come on. It's not every day we get to dress up and go to a renaissance faire."

"Especially one called Winter's Web," Finn chimed in. "How perfect is that? Why, it's like they picked an icy spider theme just for you, Gin."

I gave him a sour look, but I couldn't argue. The name was right on the nose, especially given my moniker as the Spider and the elemental Ice and Stone magic flowing through my veins.

From what I'd read online, the faire was a biannual event sponsored by the Ashland Renaissance Players, a group dedicated to showcasing all things medieval, magical, and the like. Winter's Web was the first faire of the year, with the second one to follow in the summer.

I shook my head. "I still can't believe you thought that going to a ren faire would be fun. Or that you actually bid on the tickets during a silent auction back during the holidays. Didn't you say the organizers had a ski trip to Snowline Ridge? Now, that's what *I* would have bid on. Or that spa weekend in Cypress Mountain."

"Oh, there were all kinds of trips and getaways up for grabs. I bid on several of them," Owen said. "Trust me. I know how much we could all use a vacation, especially given our latest run-in with Hugh Tucker."

Out of the corner of my eye, I spotted Finn frantically slicing his hand over his throat, not so subtly telling Owen to shut up. Owen grimaced, knowing it was too late to correct his mistake.

Saying that Hugh Tucker was my personal nemesis was putting it mildly. Tucker was the vampire enforcer of the Circle, a secret society responsible for much of the crime and corruption in Ashland. A few months ago, Tucker had tried to get me to join the Circle, and when I'd refused, he'd tried to kill me. But my relationship with the vampire was far more complicated than mere nemesis status. To my shock, I'd learned that my mother, Eira Snow, had been a member of the evil group—and that Tucker had loved her.

Tucker's feelings hadn't kept my mother from being killed on the Circle's orders, but they had led the vampire to help me more than once. Although Tucker's help always came with plenty of strings attached and usually involved him manipulating me into killing his enemies. Clever bastard.

Over the past few months, the ugly revelations about Tucker, the Circle, and my mother had just kept on coming and coming, like a freight train that kept running over the tracks of my heart no matter how hard I tried to derail it. But I'd slowly fought, clawed, and killed my way through the Circle ranks until I had finally identified the group's leader and the man ultimately responsible for the murders of my mother and my older sister, Annabella.

My uncle Mason.

That recent discovery had been a particularly surprising and brutal gut punch. My father, Tristan, had died when I was young, so I didn't remember much about him and knew nothing at all about his relatives. I was currently searching for Mason so that I could kill my mysterious uncle for everything he'd done to me and my family, but I wasn't having any luck finding him so far.

Finn kept flapping his hand at Owen, who cleared his throat, breaking the awkward silence.

"Although I have to admit that I don't remember actually bidding on the faire tickets," Owen said, changing the subject. "But at least Jo-Jo was able to find us some costumes."

"Anytime, darling," a light, feminine voice drawled. "And I think you all look fabulous."

I looked over at the middle-aged dwarf lounging on one of the cherry-red salon chairs that filled the room. Unlike the rest of us, Jolene "Jo-Jo" Deveraux wasn't wearing a costume. Instead of swaths of leather or velvet, a long white fleece housecoat patterned with tiny pink roses covered her short, stocky body. Given the early hour, her white-blond hair was still done up in pink sponge rollers, although she'd already applied her favorite pink lipstick and other makeup.

A mug of chicory coffee steamed on the table by her elbow,

and the rich, dark fumes tickled my nose and overpowered the chemical scents of the perms, hair dyes, and other products that Jo-Jo used in her beauty salon.

Despite her thick housecoat, Jo-Jo's feet were bare, and she was idly rubbing her toes back and forth over the tummy of Rosco, her beloved basset hound, who was lying on his back, with his stubby legs sticking up in the air. Every once in a while, Rosco would let out a little grunt of pleasure, but his eyes were closed, and he was fully enjoying his belly rub.

My friends and I had shown up at Jo-Jo's house about an hour ago so she could give us our costumes before she opened her salon for the day. The dwarf had also done my make-up, rimming my gray eyes with silver shadow and liner and painting my lips the same royal blue as my awful blouse. She'd also used some of her many rollers, hot irons, and combs to curl, twirl, and tease my shoulder-length dark brown hair out and up to new heights. I might be going to a renaissance faire, but this was still the South, where hair only came in two categories: big and bigger.

"At least you guys got to wear pants," another voice groused. "How did I end up in this monstrosity?"

High heels clattered on the floor, and a woman a few years younger than me stepped into the salon. She was wearing a bright, neon-pink silk dress that could best be described as *poofy*. The neckline, the sleeves, the skirt—there was some ruffle or flounce everywhere I looked. As if that wasn't bad enough, the whole thing was also covered with pale pink se-quins. They matched the ones on her pink high heels, as well as the pink crystal tiara sparkling on her head.

I wasn't the only one who had shed her usual low-key look for the ren faire. Bria Coolidge, my baby sister, might be a tough-as-nails police detective, but right now, she resembled a Southern belle princess crossed with a glittering disco ball.

Jo-Jo had also done Bria's makeup, and she'd given my

sister a soft, dreamy look, with pink shadow and silver liner that brought out her blue eyes. A matching pink gloss covered Bria's lips, and her blond hair had been set into loose waves. My sister was lovely as always, although I couldn't say the same thing about her dress.

"That is really . . . pink." That was the least offensive adjective that came to mind.

Bria glowered at me. "I know. I look like an oversize flamingo. With *ruffles*. And *sequins*."

I grinned back at her, not even trying to hide my amusement. Owen's lips twitched up into a smile as well, and Finn let out a loud snicker that had Bria planting her hands on her hips and turning her hot glower to him.

Finn's laughter abruptly cut off, and he went over and put his arm around her waist, drawing her close. "Well, I think you look smashing no matter what you wear," he said, trying to be diplomatic, since he was her significant other. "Besides, I've always had this court jester and princess fantasy . . ." He let his voice trail off and suggestively waggled his eyebrows.

Bria crinkled her nose. "Ewww."

But Finn was not deterred. He never was. He bent down and whispered something in her ear that made Bria's glower melt into a speculative look.

"Later," she murmured.

Finn kissed her cheek. Bria smiled, then reached up and flicked one of the bells on his jester's hat, making it *ting-ting-ting* out a merry tune.

Jo-Jo took a sip of her chicory coffee to hide her own smile. "I'm sorry, darling, but that was the only princess dress I could find on such short notice. There weren't many costumes to choose from, which is why your outfits don't exactly match the Renaissance period."

"It could be worse." I pointed at my own hideous shirt. "You could be wearing feathers, like me."

"At least you get to hide in the Pork Pit truck most of the day." Bria sighed and picked at one of the sequins on her poofy skirt. "I have to walk around and let people take pictures of me in this thing. Pictures that will be online *forever*. Xavier is never going to let me live this down."

Xavier was Bria's partner on the force and another one of our friends, although he was missing the faire. Lucky, lucky man.

Finn held up his hands. "Hey, it wasn't my idea to pimp us out and make us actually work at the faire. That was all Grayson's genius plan."

"As I've told you many, many times now, the Ashland Renaissance Players donate part of the proceeds from their ticket and concession sales to food banks, homeless shelters, and other charities," Owen said. "Darrell, one of the guys in my office, is really into the whole ren-faire scene. When I told him about the tickets I'd won, he said that the Renaissance Players were having trouble finding volunteers. So I thought we could help out."

I put my arm around his waist. "And that's one of the reasons I love you."

He grinned back and pulled me closer. "Don't worry. We're only volunteering for a couple of hours. We'll still have plenty of time to walk around and enjoy the faire."

"*Volunteer?*" Finn shuddered, as though the word was some awful curse. "Don't you know that I only play the part of the fool for money?"

"And here I thought you did it for free every single day," I drawled.

Finn rolled his eyes at my teasing, then turned back to the mirror and checked the bells on his jester's hat again, making sure they were perfectly draped in place.

"We need to get going," a low, eerie voice rasped. "Gotta get the truck set up."

More footsteps sounded, and another woman entered the salon. Sophia Deveraux was a dwarf like her sister, Jo-Jo, although she was much younger, with a thicker, stronger, more muscled body. Sophia was wearing a ruffled white silk shirt patterned with tiny grinning black skulls, along with black leather pants. The tops of her knee-high black leather boots were turned down, revealing the soft white interior, which was also patterned with black skulls. A large black crystal skull pendant with royal-blue heart-shaped eyes hung from her neck, while a silver cutlass dangled from her black leather belt, along with a small old-fashioned spyglass.

A white bandanna patterned with small black skulls covered her head, and the ends of her black hair had been dyed a bright blue and dusted with matching glitter. Smoky shadow rimmed Sophia's black eyes, and her lips were the same royal blue as mine.

Sophia had kicked her usual Goth style up several notches for the ren faire. The rest of us might look like we were playing dress-up, but not her. Sophia totally owned that outfit from top to bottom.

I let out a low, appreciative whistle. "Now, *that* is what a badass Goth dwarf pirate queen assassin is supposed to look like."

Sophia winked at me, then grabbed the cutlass off her belt and brandished it high in the air, as though she was calling her rowdy pirate crew to order.

"Yargh!" she cried out, shepherding us out of the salon. "To the faire!"

❊ 2 ❊

Thirty minutes later, Finn pulled his Aston Martin into a gravel parking lot, and he, Bria, Owen, and I got out of the car.

Even though it was a cold, blustery January morning, hundreds of people had still come out for the Winter's Web Renaissance Faire in Riverfront Park, and Finn had snagged one of the few remaining parking spots. We fell in with the flow of people streaming toward a black wrought-iron fence that marked the park entrance. Brightly colored ribbons had been woven through the bars, along with strings of silver bells, as if to add a bit of jingling cheer to the winter day.

Beyond the fence was a flat, grassy space that was serving as the concessions area. Food trucks, vans, and carts lined both sides of the expanse, with several wooden picnic tables and metal trash cans clustered in the middle. I focused on a white truck that featured a logo of a pig holding a platter of food, along with the words *Pork Pit* on the side. Sophia had already found a spot among the other trucks, although she wouldn't open for business until I came to help her.

Many of the other trucks, vans, and carts were already serving food, and the sticky-sweet smells of kettle corn and cotton candy curled through the air, along with the warm, rich scents of hot chocolate and cinnamon-apple cider and the harsher, greasier aromas of French fries and funnel cakes.

Finn drew in a deep appreciative breath, then sighed it out. "Ah. I love the smell of faire food in the morning."

Bria elbowed him in the side. "We're here to volunteer, remember? Not eat ourselves into a sugar coma."

Finn pouted, but then he spotted a guy dressed like a barbarian gnawing on an enormous turkey leg, and he perked right back up again. "I am *totally* getting one of those for lunch."

Bria rolled her eyes, while Owen and I laughed. We walked through the concessions area and stopped, staring out at the scene before us.

As its name implied, Riverfront Park fronted the Aneirin River as it cut through Ashland, and the grass spread out in all directions like a dull green picnic blanket. Stone paths wound through much of the park, many of them leading to water fountains, swing sets, and more picnic tables. Several rhododendron and other bushes dotted the landscape, along with a few towering maples with bare, skeletal branches.

The east side of the park butted up against the city, with metal-and-glass skyscrapers looming just a few blocks away. Over there, a low stone wall cordoned off the grass from the river below before opening up into a wide pedestrian bridge that crossed the water and led into the downtown area.

On the west side of the park, the stone paths winnowed to dirt hiking trails that vanished into the thick brown woods. Beyond the trees, an old rust-colored barn perched on a hill in the distance, like a weary, worn-out soldier keeping watch on all the activities below.

The park itself was pretty enough, but what made it truly interesting were the people roaming around inside.

Especially since most of them were in costume.

Jesters, princesses, pirates, wizards, minstrels, witches, and more had gathered for the renaissance faire. Most of the outfits were simple—crystal tiaras, plastic swords, and black eye patches paired with store-bought velvet shirts and leather pants and boots.

But some of the ensembles were quite elaborate and hand-crafted with obvious, impressive skill, like the exquisite embroidery of winter snowflakes, spring flowers, summer suns, and autumn leaves on a sorceress's long, flowing blue cloak. Or the knight encased in a full suit of armor that featured jagged marks carved into the metal, along with streaks of red paint, as though he had barely survived being attacked by some monster with extremely sharp claws.

Even the folks who weren't dressed in bona fide costumes were still sporting superhero and other fantasy T-shirts, jackets, and hoodies, while many of the kids were waving sparkling magic wands and running around with glittery fairy wings attached to their backs.

"Well," Bria said, "at least we're not the only ones in costume."

"There is that small favor," I agreed.

Whether they were in costume or not, people were already moving from one wooden booth and tented area to the next. Vendors manned many of the booths, selling everything from old-fashioned jewelry and replica weapons to handmade soaps and perfumes, while the tents were spaces for face painting, storytelling, and other activities.

In keeping with the *Winter's Web* theme, all the booths and tents had been decorated with plastic silver snowflakes and icicles, pale blue cobwebs, and strings of white and blue fairy lights. Snowflakes, icicles, and cobwebs also decorated many of the water fountains, swing sets, and picnic tables, while lights had been wrapped around several trees and bushes. A few machines were scattered about, blowing fake flakes of white and blue snow up into the air. Despite my earlier grumblings, even I had to admit that it made for a lovely, enchanting scene.

"We just need to find Darrell, and he'll tell us where to go," Owen said.

He'd barely finished speaking when a voice rose above the chattering crowd.

"Owen! There you are!"

A forty-something man stepped around a passel of giggling teenage princesses and hurried over to us. He was tall and thin, with shaggy, sandy-brown hair, hazel eyes, and silver glasses. Like Finn, he was dressed in a green velvet shirt, along with matching pants and boots, although his outfit was much more muted and practical than my brother's striped jester costume. An old-fashioned wooden bow was strapped to the man's back, along with a black leather quiver full of arrows, as though he was some ren-faire Robin Hood.

He would have looked really cool, except for two things: the clipboard he was clutching and the white paper tag on his shirt that read *Ashland Renaissance Players, Event Staff.* The modern touches totally ruined the derring-do vibe of his costume.

Owen smiled and stepped forward to shake the other man's hand. "Hey, Darrell. Looks like you're going to have a great turnout for the faire, despite the cold weather."

"Well, it is called Winter's Web," the other man joked. "I guess it would be false advertising if it wasn't cold. Ha-ha-ha-ha."

Darrell Kline was an accountant who worked for Owen and the reason we were here. In addition to managing money, Darrell was also one of the board members of the Ashland Renaissance Players and was heavily involved in staging the faire. He had been talking to Owen about volunteering at the event ever since Owen had won the tickets.

I had met Darrell a few weeks ago at the holiday party Owen

hosted for his workers at the Pork Pit. He had seemed like a nice enough guy, but he had lit up like, well, a Christmas tree once he started talking about his passion.

Darrell was into ren faires the way people in Bigtime were into superheroes or the folks in Cloudburst Falls were into monsters. During the holiday party, he had talked my ear off about all the faires, festivals, and other events he attended in Ashland and beyond. He'd also whipped out his phone and shown me photos of the costumes, weapons, and more that he wore to the events, along with his other collectibles.

Darrell had proudly revealed that he had an entire room in his house devoted to his ren-faire treasures. One-of-a-kind this, limited-edition that, hard-to-come-by thingamabob. All his photos, items, and excited chatter had blurred together after a while, although I'd been shocked at how much some of the swords, jewelry, and costumes had cost. Darrell's taste for the finer (medieval) things in life was right up there with Finn's insatiable appetite for Fiona Fine designer suits. Then again, Darrell and Finn were far less likely to get blood on their fancy costumes and sleek suits than I was on my generic clothes. But it was their money, not mine. To each his own.

"Thanks so much for coming," Darrell said. "I know you won the tickets, but I think it's so great that you and your friends wanted to volunteer."

"Volunteer?" Finn muttered. "More like being coerced—"

Bria elbowed him in the side again, cutting off his complaint. Finn let out a strangled cough and rubbed his ribs. Darrell glanced at the two of them, but Bria gave him a bright, sunny smile, as though nothing was wrong.

Owen introduced Bria and Finn, then gestured at me. "And of course, you remember Gin from the holiday party."

Darrell faced me. He drew in a breath as though he was going to murmur a greeting, but then his hazel gaze locked onto my royal-blue blouse with its shiny black thread, winking sequins, and mounds of fluttering feathers. His eyes widened, and his lips puckered into a silent O of surprise. I sighed. I had a feeling I was going to get a lot of those looks today. Even among all the costumes here, mine was truly horrific.

Darrell quickly smiled and stretched out his hand. "Gin, it's nice to see you again."

Despite the cold air, his hand was surprisingly warm and sticky, and I had to hold back a grimace as I shook it. "You too. Have you added any new treasures to your collection lately?"

He blinked, and his head jerked back, as if the question surprised him. But after a moment, he smiled again. "Oh, just a few things. Nothing too spectacular. Although there is something here today that I have my eye on."

I smiled. "Well, I hope you get it."

"Me too," he murmured. "Me too."

Darrell stared at me a moment longer before turning back to Owen. "Actually, before we get started, I was hoping to steal you away so we could discuss the Harrison account. I want to talk about how to get the forensic accountant set up when she comes in on Monday to review the files. Your friends could check out the faire while we talk. It shouldn't take more than five or ten minutes."

Owen shook his head and clapped the other man on the shoulder. "No business today. We're here to help you, remember? We can talk about the account audit when we're back in the office on Monday."

Darrell nodded. "Okay, then. First things first. We ask that volunteers turn off their phones while they're working so that they can really focus on the crowd. It also helps to promote the magical atmosphere."

"Turn off my phone? Kill me now," Finn muttered.

Bria drew back her arm like she was going to elbow him again. Finn knew when he was beaten, and he quickly side-stepped her, pulled his phone out of his pocket, and powered it down. The rest of us turned off our phones as well.

Darrell nodded again and looked at his clipboard. "Okay, let's get you guys to your stations."

We followed him deeper into the park. In addition to the booths and tents, several small wooden stages had been set up so that minstrels, magicians, jugglers, and others could perform. Soft strains of music floated through the air, along with appreciative cheers, claps, and whistles.

But the pièce de résistance was the ship.

Well, it wasn't an actual ship but rather an enormous stage that had been built to look like the deck of a ship, complete with a wooden railing, a brass steering wheel, and several small cannons. People dressed like sailors were scurrying around, checking the ropes and pulleys that hung across the stage like thick brown spiderwebs, as though they were preparing the vessel to set sail. In the center of the deck, a woman was hoisting a traditional skull-and-crossbones flag up the main mast.

"Is that a pirate ship?" Bria asked.

Darrell beamed at her. "It is. Well, not a real ship, of course. I couldn't get one of those." His lips puckered in disappointment. "But the highlight of the faire is our noon show, where the beautiful Pirate Queen Celeste will fight the evil Captain Walls."

"It sounds like quite a production," Finn said.

Darrell beamed again. "Oh, it is. You guys don't want to miss it. But for right now, let's get you settled."

We dropped Bria off at Princess Penelope's Pink Wardrobe, a tented area where children could try on everything from princess dresses to tiaras to fairy wings. Several kids were getting their faces painted, while others were running around with plastic swords and shields, as though they were gallant knights in search of monsters to slay.

A couple of little girls squealed with delight when they caught sight of Bria. "Look! Look!" one of them shouted. "It's Princess Penelope!"

Bria smiled and stepped forward to talk to the girls.

Next, Darrell led us over to the Jesters Court, another tented area, which was full of, you guessed it, jesters. Men and women wearing costumes similar to Finn's were juggling balls, engaging in acrobatics, performing pratfalls, and generally making fools of themselves, much to the delight and laughter of the onlookers.

"Oh, Finn," I drawled. "You're going to fit right in here."

My brother gave me a dirty look. "You owe me dinner at Underwood's for this humiliation."

I waggled my fingers at him. "Go on, now. Have fun."

Finn glowered at me another moment, but he plastered a smile on his face, stepped into the court, and started hamming it up with the other jesters. Despite his horror of volunteering and turning off his phone, he really was a good sport.

Darrell checked something off on his clipboard, then gestured at Owen and me. "This way, guys."

He led us back to the front of the park and over to a large open-air pavilion that was close to the food trucks. A makeshift forge had been set up inside, and a couple of blacksmiths were already hammering away and demonstrating how horseshoes, swords, and other items had been made back in the olden days. It was the perfect spot for Owen, who was a metal elemental and had his own forge at home, where he crafted all sorts of weapons, including the five silverstone knives I was wearing.

"I thought this would be right up your alley," Darrell said.

Owen grinned. "You know me too well."

Darrell grinned back at him, then turned to me. "And Gin, you're manning the Pork Pit food truck with your friend Sophia."

"That's right."

He nodded and checked off something else on his clipboard.

"Perfect. I need to go back to the main stage to help set up for the noon show, but I'll try to swing back around later to see how you guys are doing. Okay?"

Owen and I both nodded, and Darrell moved off into the crowd, still clutching his clipboard.

"Hear ye! Hear ye!" a loud voice boomed out, drawing my attention. "The Pirate Queen Celeste has arrived, along with her royal court!"

People stepped back, and a woman strode forward. She was quite beautiful, with hazel eyes and glossy black hair that had been wound up into a crownlike braid that arched across her head. She was dressed in blood-red leather from head to toe, and the tight garments showed off her muscled body and generous curves. I might have looked like a laughable pretender in my dead-bird blouse, but Celeste truly resembled a fearsome pirate queen.

A silver tiara glittered on her head, while two silver swords with large rubies set into their hilts hung from her red leather belt. Thanks to my elemental Stone magic, I could hear the gems singing about how real, pretty, and expensive they were. Seemed like Darrell wasn't the only one who spent a fortune on ren-faire treasures.

Several people dressed in red velvet shirts, pants, and gowns were following Celeste, and they smiled and waved to the crowd, as though they were real royal lords and ladies. But my gaze skipped past them and landed on the giants at the tail end of Celeste's entourage—tall, strong giants clad in black leather shirts, pants, and boots. Most of the knights, barbarians, and other costumed characters were carrying plastic weapons, but not these guys. I could tell by the way their silver swords glinted in the sunlight that the blades were the real deal.

Pirate Queen Celeste stopped in an open space on the grass, grabbed her two swords off her belt, and started twirling them around and around in her hands, putting on an impromptu show.

She definitely knew what she was doing, and she spun the blades around with smooth, easy grace. A minute later, she stabbed both of her swords high up into the air, finishing her flashy routine. People clapped and cheered, and Celeste bowed low, acknowledging their applause. Then she straightened up, holstered her swords, and started posing for pictures.

Owen noticed my curious look. "Darrell said that the pirate queen roams around the faire, showing off her sword skills, judging the jesters, crowning knights, stuff like that. It's just a way to make the event more fun and to get people excited about the noon show."

"And what about the giants?" I asked, jerking my head in their direction.

"I think they're supposed to be the pirate queen's personal guard."

A couple of the giants did stay close to Celeste, but the rest moved away and started roaming through the crowd.

"What are they doing?" I asked. "Why aren't the giants staying with the queen if they're supposed to be her guards?"

"Oh, Darrell told me that he hired some giants to work security."

I frowned. "Why would you need so much security at a ren faire?"

Owen shrugged. "Darrell said that folks can drink a little too much at the ale garden. They also had problems with people challenging each other to duels and real fights breaking out at the summer faire last year, so he thought it would be a good idea to have some giants around for this one. But he didn't want to make a big deal about it, so he had them dress up like the pirate queen's guards. Nothing to worry about."

I eyed one of the giants as he walked past us. That was a very strong giant carrying a very real and very sharp sword. In my experience, that was *plenty* to worry about.

"I should go to the forge and get started. I'll come over to the Pork Pit truck later, and we'll watch the noon show. Okay?"

I dipped into a low curtsy, with my hand pressed to my heart, as though I was a courtly lady. "As my humble blacksmith wishes."

Owen laughed. I straightened up, and the two of us shared a quick kiss. Owen winked at me, then headed toward the forge. I watched him go with a smile on my face, but I couldn't quite ignore the cold finger of unease that slid down my spine.

Perhaps it was my constant paranoia, but I couldn't help thinking that something wasn't quite right here—and that we were already trapped in Winter's Web.

I waited until Owen was safely ensconced in the forge with the other blacksmiths, then headed over to the concessions area.

By this point, almost all the food trucks, vans, and carts were open, and people were already standing in line to get everything from gourmet tacos to old-fashioned cheeseburgers to homemade ice cream, despite the cold weather.

The Pork Pit truck was parked at an angle across from the blacksmith forge on the far side of the picnic tables. In keeping with the ren-faire spirit, Sophia had hung out a large piece of poster board with the words *Ye Olde Pork Pit* written in fancy cursive with thick black marker. She'd also decorated the board with black skulls and silver hearts stuck in royal-blue cobwebs. I grinned. More like *Ye Olde Goth Pork Pit*.

The food truck had been Sophia's idea, a way for us to get out and about in the community and remind people about the good food we cooked at the restaurant. I had bought the truck and given it to her as a Christmas present, and she'd been cleaning and fixing it up ever since. We hadn't had a chance to try it out yet, and the faire was going to be our test run.

I knocked on the back door, and Sophia unlocked it. The inside of the Pork Pit food truck was like any other. A sink, a refrigerator, a freezer, a couple of stoves, several cabinets and drawers, lots of cooking gizmos, utensils, and containers. Everything you would need to make good, hot, hearty meals out of the back of a truck.

Sophia handed me a black apron patterned with tiny white skulls. "You ready?" she rasped.

I eagerly tied on the apron, since it helped to cover up my dead-bird blouse. "Let's get cooking."

Sophia rolled up the metal cover on the service window, and we were officially open for business. We'd done a lot of prep work last night at the restaurant, and Sophia started heating things up, while I sliced potatoes, onions, cabbage, and carrots.

We were going with a limited menu—pulled beef, pork, and chicken drenched in Fletcher's secret sweet-and-spicy barbecue sauce and piled high on Sophia's warm, yummy sourdough rolls. Our sides were creamy coleslaw, baked beans, and homemade potato chips sprinkled with dill weed and blue cheese crumbles. We had also made sweet tea and cherry limeade to quench everyone's thirst and oatmeal-cherry crumbles to satisfy everyone's sweet tooth.

Finn could keep his giant turkey legs. I would much rather have Pork Pit barbecue any day of the week and twice on Sundays. And plenty of other folks agreed with me, judging by the crowd that quickly formed outside the truck.

An hour later, after that initial rush, Sophia and I finally had some time to relax. Sophia made another batch of coleslaw, while I hung my arms out the service window and stared out at the booths and tents. The faire really was something to see, and I found myself smiling as I watched the people ambling around in their colorful costumes.

At least, I was smiling until I spotted the giants.

They were still roaming around the park, looking tall, strong, and intimidating in their black leather. But what truly caught my attention was the fact that the giants had their hands on the silver swords hooked to their belts, as though they were old-fashioned executioners about to whip out their blades and strike down anyone who displeased them.

Oh, I knew that the giants were probably just doing their jobs as members of the security staff. Or maybe they were playing their parts to the fullest and were determined not to break their gruff, dangerous characters during the faire.

Or maybe, just maybe, they were up to something.

Stop it, Gin! I mentally chided myself. *Stop it! Stop looking for trouble around every corner!*

Finn often said that I was totally paranoid, and he was absolutely right in his assessment. Even here, at a fun, innocent faire, I couldn't fully relax. Because this was Ashland, and someone was *always* up to something shady here. Most of the time, it was me. Maybe that was why I was always so worried—because I knew all the bad, deadly things that I'd gotten away with as the Spider when no one was looking.

"Something wrong?" Sophia rasped, now squeezing some limes and pouring their juice in a pitcher.

"Nope," I said in a breezy tone. "Just people-watching."

She eyed me a moment, clearly not believing me, but she went back to her limes.

I might not have shared my worries about the giants with Sophia, but I couldn't stop myself from tracking the men as they moved from one tent, booth, and area to the next. They didn't do anything overtly suspicious, but they didn't make an effort to participate in the faire activities either, and they didn't play to the crowd or pose for pictures like the other costumed characters were doing. It was almost like they were waiting for something to happen before they revealed their true intentions.

But what trouble could they possibly cause at a ren faire? Steal the more expensive swords and jewelry? Crack some skulls and make off with people's wallets and phones? Swipe the cash from the food trucks? Each new possibility that popped into my mind only increased my worry.

A few of the giants wandered by the Pork Pit truck, and one of them stopped and peered up at me. He was taller than the other giants and quite handsome, with golden hair, tan skin, and pale blue eyes.

I smiled at him, trying to be friendly and not paranoid, but he gave me a flat stare and moved on.

That giant and two others rounded the side of the blacksmith forge and disappeared. They might have been out of sight, but they were definitely not out of my mind—

A light trill of laughter caught my ear, interrupting my thoughts.

Pirate Queen Celeste's royal rounds had finally taken her over to the blacksmith forge, and she was standing next to Owen, who was showing her a dagger he'd made. Owen also showed the blade to the other people gathered around and answered a few questions. Once he was finished, everyone in the crowd clapped in appreciation, then moved on to check out the rest of the faire.

Everyone except Celeste.

The lords and ladies in her court drifted away to browse through the soaps, perfumes, and more in some nearby booths. But not Celeste. She sidled closer to Owen and smiled, clearly interested in all the wares he had to offer. Seemed I wasn't the only one who was into humble blacksmiths.

She said something, but Owen immediately shook his head and stepped away, turning down her proposal. Celeste smiled again and shrugged, as if to say there were no hard feelings.

Owen nodded, then moved away. Celeste stared at him a moment longer, her red lips puckered in thought, then headed back into the crowd. The lords and ladies left their browsing behind and followed her, playing their parts again. A couple of the giants trailed after them as well, their hands still on their swords.

Owen saw me watching them and jogged across the grass to me.

"What was that about?" I asked.

"Oh, Her Majesty Celeste was wondering if I could make a custom set of swords for her, but I told her that I just craft weapons for myself these days. And for my favorite Spider, of course." He winked at me.

I smiled back at him. Owen always knew just what to say to make me feel better. Still, something about Celeste and the giants made me uneasy.

"It's almost time for the noon show, if my pirate queen assassin will let this humble blacksmith escort her to the stage." Owen grinned and bowed low.

My smile widened. "This pirate queen assassin would like that very much."

Sophia and I closed up the Pork Pit truck and hung out a sign saying that we would be back after the show. Then Owen offered us each an arm, and we strolled over to the main stage.

Almost everyone in the park had gathered here for the show, including Finn and Bria. Finn was chomping down on a giant turkey leg, with grease already smeared all over his face, while Bria had a funnel cake topped with fresh blackberries and raspberries and generously dusted with powdered sugar. She was using a fork to daintily cut into and then eat her fried treat, just like a proper princess would.

I waved at them, and they toasted me with their food.

"Here we go," Owen murmured, drawing my attention back to the stage.

Darrell Kline strolled out to the middle of the pirate ship

deck. As if on cue, the wind picked up just enough to flutter the black flag with its white skull-and-crossbones that topped the main mast.

Darrell was still clutching his clipboard and wearing his green velvet Robin Hood costume. He smiled and waved, and everyone quieted down.

"Thank you so much for stepping back in time with us today." He beamed at the crowd. "On behalf of the Ashland Renaissance Players and all our volunteers, sponsors, and vendors, we're so happy that you decided to get tangled up in Winter's Web. Ha-ha-ha-ha."

No one really laughed at his joke, so Darrell cleared his throat and moved on. "And now, ladies and gentlemen, for your entertainment . . . the Pirate Queen Celeste and her Marvelous Marauders!"

Darrell swept his hand out to the side, then hurried off the stage. The second he disappeared, Celeste strolled into view. She plucked her two silver swords out of their scabbards and went through a much longer, more detailed routine than what she'd done in the park earlier. The crowd started *oohing* and *aahing*, and Celeste grinned and spun her swords even faster.

Maybe it was my imagination or some trick of the noon sun, but it almost seemed like the weapons were sparking and glowing in her hands, and I could have sworn that I felt a faint gust of *real* magic in the air. My eyes narrowed, but Celeste was spinning, whirling, and twirling her body and blades around so fast that I couldn't quite tell what, if any, elemental power she might have.

A cheery sea shanty started playing, and a plethora of pirates raced into view. In an instant, they had swarmed all over the stage, standing on the railing, hanging off the netting, and even scaling the main mast up to the crow's nest at the very top. They rose and fell on ropes and pulleys and did somersaults and other tricks that had the kids squealing with delight.

After that initial blast of action, the music died down, and Celeste and the pirates put on a brief play. The story revolved around the villainous Captain Walls trying to take Celeste's ship, but it was really just an excuse for Celeste to show off her sword skills again by defeating the other pirate in one-on-one combat.

Several characters also gave long-winded, flowery speeches about doing one's duty, living by the pirate's code, and dying with honor—usually right before they were forced to walk the plank to meet a grisly death at the teeth of the sharks supposedly swimming below. The two rival crews also clashed in a massive final battle, and they even set off the cannons, which belched out loud, thunderous *booms* and thick plumes of black smoke.

All put together, it was a fun, lively, impressive show, and I smiled and clapped along to the jaunty music with everyone else.

Thirty minutes later, the show ended, and Celeste and the pirates joined hands, walked to the front of the stage, and took a well-deserved bow. The performers smiled and took another bow, soaking up the enthusiastic applause.

Several kids ran up to the bottom of the stage and held out faire flyers, and the performers, including Celeste, left the stage and came down to autograph the papers and pose for pictures.

Darrell hurried back out to the middle of the stage, still clutching his clipboard. "Be sure to come back for our three o'clock show!" he yelled, although no one paid any attention to him as they drifted away from the stage and back over to the booths and tents.

I turned to Sophia and Owen. "That was actually really cool."

"You sound surprised," Owen said.

I shrugged. "I didn't know what to expect."

Sophia jerked her thumb over her shoulder. "Back to work?"

"Yeah, I'm right behind you."

She nodded and headed toward the concessions area.

Owen held out his arm to me again. "Shall I escort my pirate queen assassin back to her own ship?"

I laughed and threaded my arm through his. "I don't think the food truck would float very well, but escort me, you may."

He grinned, laid his hand over mine, and gently squeezed my fingers. I curled my fingers into his and squeezed back—

I spotted a flash of silver out of the corner of my eye, so I looked in that direction. Pirate Queen Celeste was twirling one of her swords around in her hand again.

And she was watching me.

Celeste kept spinning her sword around in a smooth, lazy motion as though it was a baton instead of a deadly weapon. She realized that I was watching her watch me and did an elaborate flourish with the blade before bowing low. The gesture was more mocking than not. Then she straightened up, slid her sword back into its scabbard, and turned to sign a little girl's flyer.

Celeste didn't look at me again, but I couldn't help but feel like she was still aware of me, the same way that I was aware of her.

"Gin? Is something wrong?" Owen asked.

I focused on him. "Nope, nothing at all. Escort away."

He led me away from the stage. I didn't look back, but I would have bet that Celeste was watching us again—and that her interest in me was far from casual.

✿ 4 ✿

Owen escorted me back to the Pork Pit truck. He had to
give another demonstration, but we made plans to meet
up later to check out the rest of the faire.

I kissed him on the cheek and watched to make sure that he
got back to the blacksmith forge okay. Then I knocked on the
door, and Sophia let me into the truck.

Sophia and I hit another busy patch, and I spent the next
hour dishing up barbecue, sweet tea, and oatmeal-cherry crumbles before the crowd finally died down again.

"Are you okay here by yourself for a little while?" I asked.
"Owen should be done with his demonstration by now, and he
wanted to explore the faire."

Sophia grunted, which was her way of saying *yes*, and put
another pot of baked beans on one of the burners to simmer. I
pulled off my apron and hung it on a hook on the wall before
opening the back door of the truck and stepping outside.

I had started to head over to the blacksmith forge when a
sharp jerk of movement caught my eye. I looked to my right.

The blond giant I'd seen earlier was sitting at a nearby picnic
table, along with two other men. Ostensibly, the three giants

were taking a break from their security duties and eating lunch, given the drinks, containers, and crumpled napkins clustered around them. But all three men were trying very hard not to stare at me, and they all had their hands on their swords, even though the blades were lying out flat on the table.

I stayed where I was and pulled my phone out of the back pocket of my leather pants, pretending to check my messages, even though I'd turned the device off earlier. All the while, though, I discreetly watched the three giants.

They got up from the table and slid their swords back into their scabbards. Then they took their drinks, containers, and napkins over to a trash can and dumped their food into the garbage, even though they'd barely touched their cheeseburgers and fries.

That vague, uneasy dread I'd been feeling all day solidified into cold certainty. The giants hadn't been interested in their food. Not at all. It had just been an excuse so they could sit by the Pork Pit truck and keep an eye on me.

Why? What did they want? Had Hugh Tucker sent them? Maybe Uncle Mason had finally realized that I was on to him and had dispatched some goons to eliminate me. Or maybe they were working for another one of my many enemies, like Jonah McAllister. It could be any one of those things or another possibility that I hadn't even considered yet.

I glanced around, wondering if my friends had clocked the giants. Sophia was busy helping some customers, while Owen was still over at the forge, showing a little girl the four-leaf clover he'd made. I didn't see Bria or Finn anywhere, but they were probably still at their princess and jester stations deeper in the park.

I didn't want to bother my friends, so I decided to go it alone. There were only three giants. That was hardly a workout after Alanna Eaton, Bruce Porter, and some of the other vicious folks I'd battled recently.

Besides, I was the only one who should have to get blood on her costume today.

So I slid my phone back into my pocket, then strolled away from the Pork Pit truck. Instead of going into the crowded park, I veered in the opposite direction, heading toward one of the dirt hiking trails that led into the woods. I smiled and nodded at the people I passed, but I quickly left the noise, crowd, and commotion of the faire behind and stepped into the trees.

Time to see if the giants would follow the Spider into her own Winter's Web.

I ambled along the trail as though I didn't have a care in the world. No clouds marred the clear blue canvas of the sky, although the weak winter sun did little to drive away the perpetual chill in the air. Trees rose all around me, their bare brown branches making them look like skeleton sentinels silently studying me. A few hardy evergreen bushes also dotted the landscape, along with small patches of ice and snow that were tucked back in the dappled shadows. The rich, dark scents of the earth and dried leaves filled the air, and I drew in a breath, letting the aromas wash away the fried-food stench of the faire.

It would have been a lovely, quiet walk—if I wasn't being followed.

I didn't hear footsteps behind me, but that didn't really mean anything, so I waited until I reached a bend in the trail, then discreetly glanced back over my shoulder.

Through the trees, I spotted the three giants on the trail a couple hundred feet behind me. They were definitely following me.

Worst mistake they'd ever made.

I kept going at my slow, steady pace, looking for a good spot to confront my enemies. Once I found it, I could slip off the trail, come up behind the men, and make them tell me who had sent them. And if it was Hugh Tucker or dear Uncle Mason, then I would use the giants—and their bodies—to send a bloody message right back to the Circle.

So I headed deeper into the woods, as though I didn't even notice the three giants creeping along behind me. A couple of minutes later, the trail turned again and led to a stone bridge that arched over a small, gurgling creek that trickled off from the nearby Aneirin River. I quickly scanned the area, then grinned. Perfect.

I held up my hand and waved. "Owen!" I called out in a loud voice. "Hey, Owen! Wait for me!"

And then I picked up my pace, jogging away from the giants. I discreetly glanced back over my shoulder again.

The giants hadn't been expecting my outburst or my sudden surge of speed, and they stopped, not sure if they should keep pretending they weren't following me or give up the ghost and chase after me. I increased my speed, rounding another bend in the trail and leaving them completely behind. The moment the giants were out of sight, I sprinted toward the bridge. I only had a few seconds to get into place.

I ran all the way across the bridge and darted around one side of the railing. I quickly jogged down the cold, frozen creek bank, then plastered myself up against one of the gray stone supports so that I was standing underneath the far right corner of the bridge.

I glanced up through the railing. I didn't have the best angle, but the view was good enough to let me see the giants racing toward the bridge. Their shouts drifted down to me.

"Where did she go?"

"I don't see her!"

"We can't lose her!"

All three giants ran onto the bridge, each one now clutching a sword in his hand. Whoever the giants were, they didn't want me to leave the woods alive.

They just didn't realize that I felt the exact same way about them.

I palmed one of my silverstone knives, curling my fingers around the hilt so that the spider rune stamped into the metal pressed into the larger matching scar embedded in my palm. The sensation comforted and steadied me the way it always did.

I studied the giants, plotting the best way to take them down. Normally, I would have just dived into the pack and hacked and slashed my way through them until they were all dead. But we were still fairly close to the ren faire, and I didn't want anyone to hear the men's screams and come to investigate—or worse, call the police. No, this needed to be done as quietly as possible.

Good thing quietly was one of my specialties.

"Let's split up," the golden-haired giant suggested. "She can't have gotten far. Arthur, you come with me. We'll check the trail and the woods up ahead. Galahad, you stay here in case she comes back this way."

Galahad nodded. "Got it, Lancelot."

Lancelot? Arthur? Galahad? And here I thought the Knights of the Round Table were supposed to be the good guys. Seemed like the giants were determined to stay in character right up until they killed me.

The three giants split up. Lancelot and Arthur jogged off the bridge and back out onto the trail, disappearing deeper into the woods. Galahad stayed behind, his head snapping back and forth in time to his quick, worried pacing.

"Where are you?" Galahad muttered. "Where are you?"

He kept pacing back and forth, his boots *snap-snap-snap-snapping* against the flagstones. But he quickly grew tired of that and headed toward the opposite side of the bridge, as though he was going to check the trail we'd all used to get here.

I waited until his back was to me, then eased around the

support, climbed up the creek bank, and crouched down beside the bridge.

I paused a moment, but Galahad was still turned away from me, so I tightened my grip on my knife, got to my feet, and sidled forward, determined to bury my blade in his back before he realized what was happening.

But I wasn't quite quick enough.

Galahad must have heard the soft *thud-thud-thud-thud* of my footsteps, or perhaps he spotted my shadow slinking up on the bridge beside him. Either way, he turned around before I could strike.

Galahad sucked in a breath, probably to scream for his friends. Not very brave or knightly of him. I surged forward, closed the distance between us, and sliced my knife across his neck. The giant let out a choked, bloody gurgle, then pitched forward and landed in the middle of the bridge with a loud, heavy *thump*.

"Hey! There she is!"

"Get her!"

I whirled around.

Lancelot and Arthur must have realized that I hadn't gone deeper into the woods, because they'd doubled back. They raised their swords and rushed onto the bridge. I growled, palmed another knife, and stepped up to meet them.

Clash!

Clash-clash!

Clash!

Lancelot and Arthur swung their swords at me over and over again. I spun, whirled, and twirled between the two men, using my knives to keep their blades from cutting into me. But the giants were much bigger and stronger, and their arms and swords gave them a much longer reach than I had with my knives. Despite all my years as an assassin, I barely managed to keep the giants from skewering me.

I blocked an attack from Arthur, but Lancelot came up beside me and lashed out with his sword. I twisted my body to the side, avoiding most of the blow, but the edge of his blade still sliced across my left forearm, opening up a deep gash.

I hissed and staggered back, moving away from the giants and their swords.

"Not so tough now, are you, Spider?" Lancelot sneered, twirling his sword around in his hand.

Arthur grinned and did the same thing. Then the two of them advanced on me again. I was really starting to hate these so-called knights.

My gaze snapped back and forth, flicking from one giant to the other and back again. Despite their heavy swords, the two men were barely winded thanks to their great strength, but I was sucking down air, trying to get my breath back after using so much energy to block their hard, furious attacks. My knives weren't going to get the job done, not in this situation, so I tucked them back up my sleeves.

"Aw, are you giving up already, little Spider?" Lancelot sneered at me again. "If you raise your hands and surrender, we might just do you a favor and kill you quickly. Give you an honorable death, at least."

An honorable death? There was no such fucking thing. These guys had been hanging around the ren faire too long. All those pretty proclamations and flowery words about honor, codes, and duty had addled their minds—and were going to get them killed in another minute, two tops.

I smiled at him. "You want me to raise my hands? You got it, Sir Knight."

I reached for my magic, snapped up my hands, and flung a spray of Ice daggers out at them. Given their big, strong bodies and thick, heavy leather outfits, the daggers didn't have much chance of hurting the giants, but Lancelot and Arthur didn't realize that, and they both yelped in surprise, lifted their arms, and turned away from my frosty blast of magic.

The sharp shards of elemental Ice splintered against their massive biceps and shoulders and dropped harmlessly to the ground, but the giants' distraction let me close the distance between us. I went left, targeting Lancelot first, since he was the better fighter and far more dangerous than Arthur. I leaped up, grabbed hold of the bridge railing, and kicked out, slamming my boot into his sword hand.

Lancelot yelped, staggered back, and dropped his weapon.

Arthur snarled, stepped up, and swung his blade at me, but I avoided his vicious blow, darted forward, and scooped Lancelot's sword up off the bridge.

The weapon was far, far heavier than I'd expected it to be. I had to wrap both hands around the hilt, but I managed to hoist it up. Arthur raised his sword high overhead, giving me an easy opening, and I stepped up, whirled around, and sliced the stolen blade across his stomach.

The giant screamed and staggered back against the railing. Arthur's feet flew out from under him, and he collapsed to the ground. His sword dropped from his hand and skittered across the flagstones, shooting off a few hot silver sparks.

Arthur's panicked gaze dropped to his stomach, and he clamped his hands over the deep, gruesome wound, trying to keep his blood and guts from leaking out. I could have told him that it was a losing battle and not to bother, but I went for the more direct approach of lashing out with my sword again. This time, I buried the blade in the side of the giant's neck, cutting off his screams.

I tried to yank the sword free so that I could turn my attention back to Lancelot, but I couldn't quite manage it. I grunted and tried again, but the blade was firmly stuck in Arthur, like, well, a sword in a stone.

"You bitch!" Lancelot screamed. "You killed him!"

The giant charged at me, his arms outstretched like he wanted to wrap me up in a bear hug and crush me to death. I couldn't let that happen, so I let go of the sword and lurched away from Arthur. But once again, I wasn't quite quick enough, and Lancelot plowed into me. I barely had time to grab hold of my Stone magic to harden my skin into an impenetrable shell before the giant body-slammed me down onto the bridge. Despite my Stone magic, the bruising blow still hurt, and I let out a low groan of pain.

"You bitch!" he screamed again, wrapping his hands around my throat. "You killed them!"

Lancelot started squeezing my neck, trying to choke me to death. At the same time, he lifted my shoulders and chest up off the bridge, getting ready to slam my head back against the stone, probably over and over again until he cracked my skull open like an egg.

I couldn't let that happen either, so I reached for even more of my Stone magic. There was no time to be subtle, so I focused on the closest part of the bridge railing. Then I lashed out with my magic, hammering my Stone power into the supports the way Owen and the other blacksmiths had been hammering their weapons and other metal creations in the forge earlier.

CRACK!

Several pieces of stone exploded out of the railing. I put a lot of magic into the blast, and one of the chunks zipped across the open space and hit Lancelot in the side of his neck. The giant let out a choked cry. He toppled off me and flopped over onto his back, wheezing and clutching his throat.

I sucked down some much-needed air, then forced myself to roll over and get back up onto my knees. I palmed a knife and loomed over Lancelot, ready to drive the blade into his ribs if he came at me again, but I didn't have to.

I'd already killed him with my Stone magic.

That chunk of railing hadn't just made Lancelot choke and gasp for air. Part of the stone had shattered and driven itself deep into his neck, wounding him just as badly as my knife would have. A steady stream of blood was pouring down his throat, and it had already started pooling around his head like he was lying on a scarlet cloak.

I leaned over the giant and fisted my hand in the front of his leather shirt, shaking him and trying to get him to focus on me before he bled out.

"Who sent you?" I hissed. "Was it Tucker? Mason? Are they here? Are they watching us right now?"

But I'd done too good a job with my Stone magic, and it was too late to get any answers from Lancelot. The giant gurgled and stretched up an arm like he was going to shove me away, but his strength gave out, and his hand flopped back down onto the bridge. A moment later, his body sagged, and his blue eyes became fixed and frozen.

A knight no more, Lancelot was dead.

✻ 5 ✻

I slumped down on the bridge beside the dead giant, still trying to get my breath back, even as I scanned the surrounding woods.

The fight hadn't been nearly as quiet as I'd wanted it to be, but I didn't see anyone running through the trees, and I didn't hear any shouts that would indicate that someone had heard the giants' yells and screams and was coming to investigate.

Since I was relatively safe, at least for the moment, I glanced at the three giants, but they all lay where they had fallen, as dead as dead could be. They couldn't give me any answers about who had sent them and why.

But maybe their phones could.

I got up on my knees again, tucked my knife back up my sleeve, and started patting down Lancelot. Despite the fact that he was gussied up in black leather for the faire, he still had his phone in his pants pocket, and it was still on. The honorable knight had done the not-so-honorable thing of ignoring Darrell's request to turn it off. Luckily, the device hadn't been damaged during our fight, and I hit the button on the side. The phone was locked, but maybe I could fix that.

I grabbed Lancelot's right hand, which was covered in blood and bruises, much like the rest of him was. The left sleeve of my dead-bird blouse was already torn from where I'd been cut during the fight, so I ripped off some of the loose fabric and used it to wipe the blood off Lancelot's index finger. Then I pressed his slightly cleaner finger onto the screen. A moment later, the device unlocked, and I let the giant's hand flop back down to the bridge.

The first thing I did was change the settings so that the phone would stay unlocked. Then I scrolled through Lancelot's contacts, but I didn't recognize any of the names. No Tucker, no Mason, no mysterious initials, although there were several odd monikers like the Mesmerizing Magician, the Red Queen, the Bloody Barbarian, and so on.

Lancelot had really been into the whole ren-faire scene. No wonder he'd been so good with that sword. He'd actually learned how to use the long, heavy blade. I made a mental note to add medieval weapons to my assassin training regimen.

Since I didn't recognize any of the contact names, I moved on to the call log. But none of the phone numbers jumped out at me, so I pulled up his texts. And I finally found something interesting.

Someone called the Black Rook had sent Lancelot several messages over the past few months. In fact, it looked like the giant had been texting with this person more than anyone else. Most of the texts were about the renaissance faire and focused on costumes, weapons, and the like. I was just about to give up and search the other two giants for their phones when I spotted a final text that was part of a new chain. So I opened it.

Target will be at Winter's Web as planned, along with friends. We need to separate and isolate the target. You know what to do.

Well, that was some pretty ominous bad-guy talk. This text also had a photo attachment, so I clicked on the file and waited for it to download and then pop up on the screen. I fully expected to see some shot of myself walking down the sidewalk or maybe even cooking inside the Pork Pit. But my smiling face wasn't the one that appeared on the screen.

It was Owen's.

I blinked and blinked, but the image didn't change. The picture looked like it had been taken at some recent charity event, given the red and green holiday lights glowing in the background. Owen was wearing a black tuxedo and grinning at someone I couldn't see, but he was most definitely the focus of the photo.

Owen? Why would the giant have a picture of Owen instead of me—

Horrible understanding slammed into my brain, while sick certainty curdled in my stomach. The giants might have been watching me, but only to make sure that I didn't interfere with their plans. This wasn't about me. For once, I didn't seem to be the main target.

Owen was.

Fear, worry, and dread punched me in the heart, one right after another, leaving me dizzy, shaking, and breathless. For a moment, everything inside me lurched to a cold, hard, painful stop. Then my mind kicked into gear again, and my body zoomed into overdrive.

I got to my feet, stuffed the giant's phone into my pants pocket, and started running.

I left the dead giants where they had fallen on the bridge. I didn't care if anyone found them and realized what had happened, that I had killed them.

Right now, the only thing that mattered was getting to Owen.

So I ran, ran, ran, as fast as I could, my boots pounding along the trail in perfect time to the frantic fear pulsing through my heart.

Must save Owen . . . must save Owen . . . must save Owen . . .

It became like a mantra running through my mind, and I used it to block out everything else. The cold air searing my lungs, the growing stitch in my side, the throbbing sting in my forearm, the blood still sliding down my skin from where Lancelot had cut me with his sword. I ignored it all, sucked down another breath, and forced myself to move even faster.

I hadn't gone as far into the woods as I'd thought, and I quickly made it back to the end of the trail. I sprinted out into the grassy park and had to stop short to let a group of boys dressed like Vikings pass by. The second they were out of the way, I started running again.

Well, I tried to run. The park was even more crowded than before, and I had to slow down to a fast walk so that I wouldn't bowl people over. Even then, I still had to pull up, sidestep, and dart around person after person after person, and I had to bite my tongue to keep from screaming at each and every delay.

I finally made it back to the concessions area. Sophia was still inside the Pork Pit truck, and she leaned out the window as I raced by, obviously wondering what going on, but I didn't have time to stop and explain.

Must save Owen . . . must save Owen . . . must save Owen . . .

The mantra kept pounding in my head, getting a little louder, quicker, and more frantic with each passing second, and I hurried across the grass and over to the blacksmith forge.

A large crowd was gathered around the front of the forge for the latest demonstration. I stood on my tiptoes, but I couldn't see if Owen was leading the event, and I couldn't hear his voice over the loud, constant hammering. So I skirted around the edge of the crowd, then zipped through a gap between two people. Eventually, I wound up on the left side of the forge.

It wasn't as crowded back here, and I spotted a guy in the

rear wearing a black leather cap and using a hammer to shape a red-hot sword. Relief filled me, but I forced myself to wait until he'd plunged the blade into a trough of water before I hurried over to him.

I grabbed his arm and turned him around. "Owen! I'm so glad I found you—"

The words died on my lips, and my relief was snuffed out just like the heat from the sword had been in the water.

It wasn't Owen.

The blacksmith stared at me, obviously wondering who I was and why I was babbling about some guy named Owen.

I dropped his arm, stepped back, and gave him a sheepish grimace. "Sorry. I thought you were someone else."

The guy shrugged, accepting my apology, and went back to work.

I turned around, scanning the area. Another blacksmith was at the front of the forge, although he'd finally stopped the loud hammering and was now explaining his process to the crowd. A couple of other blacksmiths were also working on their own projects. Kids were running around, while their parents were admiring the weapons, horseshoes, and other items on display. Everything was perfectly normal except for one thing: I didn't see Owen anywhere.

"Owen!" I called out. "Owen!"

No answer.

I was getting more and more worried and more and more desperate, so I went around to the back of the forge, hoping that he was taking a break. But of course, he wasn't out here either.

I looked out into the park beyond, but it was more of the same. Kids playing, adults shopping, costumed characters posing for pictures.

No Owen.

I turned around in a slow circle, just in case I'd missed

anything, but I hadn't. I stepped forward and opened my mouth to call out to him again, and my boot scuffed across something on the grass.

A black leather cap with long ear flaps was lying on the ground—the same sort of hat that Owen had been wearing.

Icy dread flooded my heart, but I crouched down and picked up the cap. The leather was crumpled, as though it had been snatched off someone's head, thrown down, and then stomped on for good measure. Part of the leather looked a bit darker and shinier than the rest, so I rubbed my fingers over that spot. Sticky moisture clung to my skin in a sickening, familiar sensation. I froze a moment, then slowly pulled my hand up where I could see it.

Faint smears of blood were streaked across my fingertips.

I sucked in a ragged breath, even as more and more worry shot through my body.

Owen was gone.

✦ 6 ✦

*A*s much as I wanted to surge to my feet, run around, and scream Owen's name, I forced myself to calmly, slowly, carefully examine the ground where I'd found his hat.

The grass had been flattened in patches and churned up in others, along with the dirt underneath, indicating a struggle. Owen had come here for some reason, or had been lured here, and then he'd been attacked. In addition to being a metal elemental, Owen was also a good, strong fighter. Even if he'd been taken by surprise, he still would have put up a fierce struggle, and all the flattened grass and disturbed earth told me that he'd been attacked by at least a couple of guys. Probably more of the black-leather-clad giants.

With a heavy heart, I also forced myself to search the ground for more blood, but thankfully, the smears on Owen's cap were all I found.

I stood up, thinking about what I knew. Owen had definitely been attacked here and then taken somewhere else. Despite the crowds, a snatch-and-grab would have been easy enough to pull off. A couple of the costumed giants could have bashed

Owen over the head and carted him off in plain sight simply by making the whole thing seem like an act and part of the ren-faire fun instead of the kidnapping it truly was.

And it *was* a kidnapping. If someone had just wanted to kill Owen, they could have shoved a knife in his back and left his body here. But there was no body, which told me that Owen was still alive.

For now.

But why kidnap him? Was this some ploy by Hugh Tucker to get leverage over me? To force me to kill another one of the vampire's Circle enemies? And why grab Owen at the faire with so many potential witnesses around? Why not snatch him when he was coming out of his office late one night? Or from his house, where there was far less chance of someone realizing what was going on?

My hand fisted tight around the bloody leather cap. I didn't know the answers to my questions, but I was damn sure going to find them out.

And when I found the people who had taken Owen, they were the ones who were going to fucking *bleed*.

Still clutching Owen's hat, I skirted around the blacksmith forge, threaded my way through the crowd, and hurried back over to the Pork Pit truck. Sophia had fed the latest wave of customers, and she leaned out the window again, a concerned look on her face.

"What's wrong?" she rasped.

I quickly told her about the giants following me into the woods and then handed her Owen's bloody hat.

Sophia studied the hat a moment, then set it aside. Her face darkened, and her black eyes glittered with anger. "What do you want me to do?"

"Call Finn and Bria—" I stopped and let out a vicious curse. Calling them wouldn't do any good, since they'd turned their phones off earlier, just like Owen and I had.

"Close up the truck, then go find Finn and Bria and tell them what's going on," I said. "Spread out and start looking for Owen. Ask around, and see if anyone remembers some giants in black leather carrying another guy. Whoever took him couldn't have gotten too far away yet."

"What are you going to do?" she rasped.

"I'm going to find another giant dressed like the ones who attacked me and squeeze him for answers. I don't know that all those giants are working together, but it's a place to start."

Sophia nodded and started closing up the truck. I left her there and hurried over to the wrought-iron fence that cordoned off the park from the gravel lot beyond. I looked out over the rows of cars, trucks, and vans, but I didn't see anything suspicious, and there were no empty spaces to indicate that a vehicle had recently left.

The kidnappers could have taken Owen out of the park, put him in a car, and driven away, but it would have been much more conspicuous, and they would have had to walk right by the Pork Pit truck to do it. Whoever had planned this had been very careful and smart so far, and I doubted they would have wanted to risk Sophia seeing and stopping them. No, my gut was telling me that Owen was still nearby.

That was my hope, anyway. I wasn't going to think about all the awful things that might have already happened, all the ways that he could have been horribly hurt and brutally tortured. My stomach roiled with fear, but I pushed it away and instead focused on the cold determination surging through me. I didn't know what this was about yet, but I *was* going to find Owen, and the people who took him *were* going to pay for what they'd done.

With that dark and deadly promise beating in my heart,

I moved away from the fence, walked back through the concessions area, and started doing a sweep of the front part of the park, searching for the black-leather-clad giants.

But I couldn't find them—not a single one.

Earlier today, the giants had been *everywhere*, but now there was nary a one in sight. That only confirmed my suspicion that they were working together. After all, why stick around the scene of your crime when you'd already abducted your victim?

Still, I kept scanning the throngs of people, desperately hoping I'd spot the giants. All I needed was one of them to talk and tell me where they'd taken Owen. Just one.

No giants magically appeared to answer my silent plea, but as I looked around, I realized that someone else was also missing from the faire.

Pirate Queen Celeste.

My head snapped back and forth, and I scanned the crowd, but I didn't see Celeste anywhere either. She had vanished, along with the giants.

Oh, I supposed that Celeste could have been taking a break, hanging out somewhere deeper in the park, or maybe even over at the stage, preparing for the next show. But mine was a suspicious mind, and I remembered how the giants had entered the faire as part of her entourage this morning, almost as if they worked for her in real life.

Maybe they did.

Even more telling was the fact that Celeste had tried to cozy up to Owen earlier at the forge. Sure, Owen had said that Celeste had wanted some custom swords, but what if that had just been an excuse to get him alone? I didn't know that I was right, but I wasn't going to take a chance that I was wrong either. Not when Owen's life was hanging in the balance.

So I quit looking for the giants and started searching for Celeste instead.

I went over to a group of people standing in front of a jewelry booth. "Excuse me, have you seen Pirate Queen Celeste?"

I didn't think a more ridiculous sentence had ever come out of my mouth. Then again, this had started out as a ridiculous day, although it had quickly turned into a bloody one—and would probably get bloodier still, before all was said and done.

Those folks shook their heads, so I moved on. I asked the same thing over and over again of all the kids, teens, and adults who crossed my path, but they all kept shaking their heads *no-no-no*. Despite the throngs of people, no one remembered seeing Celeste recently or knew where she might have gone—

I spotted a flash of red out of the corner of my eye. I whirled around in that direction, and I saw Celeste disappearing behind one of the vendor booths about twenty feet away.

I glanced around, but I didn't see Sophia, Finn, or Bria anywhere. I couldn't wait for my friends. I had to act now or risk losing Celeste, so I headed after the pirate queen.

"Hey!"

"Watch it!"

"Rude much?"

A few people let out angry mutters as I shoved past them, but I didn't dare slow down to apologize. The only thing that mattered was tracking Celeste back to Owen before it was too late.

I reached the booth where Celeste had disappeared, and I finally did slow down, creeping up to the corner and peering around the side. I didn't see Celeste or any of the giants, but the booth was close to one of the hiking trails that led into the woods on the west side of the park.

I hadn't seen any buildings or other structures during my earlier hike through the woods, but this trail was about a quarter mile away from the one that I'd used. Either way, it was the most likely place for Celeste to have gone, so I stepped around the booth, jogged over to the trail, and plunged back into the trees.

I palmed a knife and moved quickly and quietly along the path. Every once in a while, I stopped to look and listen, but I didn't see anyone on the trail ahead of me or hunkered down in the surrounding woods, and the thick tangle of trees blocked out the clatter and commotion from the faire.

A couple of hundred feet into the woods, I came across another stone bridge that arched over the same creek that I'd seen before. I approached the bridge with caution, but Celeste wasn't lying in wait underneath it to attack me like a troll, so I crossed it.

I was just about to step off the far side of the bridge when the phone in my pocket started buzzing.

I frowned, wondering why the device was buzzing instead of playing one of the ring tones that Silvio Sanchez, my personal assistant, had programmed into my phone. Silvio and I both loved movie music, and he'd downloaded a bunch of classic cinematic themes into my device.

Then I realized it wasn't my phone—it was the phone I'd taken off Lancelot.

The phone buzzed a moment longer, then fell silent. I pulled the device out of my pocket and stared at the screen. It was another message from the mysterious Black Rook.

Did you take care of the assassin?

More ominous bad-guy speak, asking if the giants had killed me yet.

I hesitated. I didn't know if Lancelot and the Black Rook were using keywords or some other code, but it would be more suspicious if there was no response, so I sent back a generic bad-guy answer.

It's done.

I waited, holding my breath and hoping I'd made the right choice. The phone buzzed again a few seconds later with another message.

Good. Meet us at the barn to get your cut.

The barn? What barn?

Then I remembered the old barn I'd seen perched on the hill beyond the woods when we first arrived at the park this morning. That must be where this trail led and where the kidnappers had taken Owen.

I switched the phone to silent, shoved it back into my pocket, and hurried along. A few hundred feet later, the path started climbing, and that old barn came into view through the trees.

As soon as I spotted the structure, I stepped off the trail and started moving from one tree to the next, steadily and silently making my way up the incline. I didn't spot Celeste or any of the giants lurking in the woods, and no trip-wires littered the ground. Sloppy, sloppy, sloppy of the kidnappers not to leave a rear guard behind or at least a few rune booby traps buried in the leaves in case someone like me came creeping up behind them.

A few minutes later, I crested the top of the hill and hunkered down behind a large boulder at the edge of the woods. The trail I'd been on before ran out of the trees and snaked through an overgrown field choked with tall grasses, winter wildflowers, and other vegetation before ending at a small mowed yard that surrounded the barn.

I studied the structure, but it looked like any other barn in the Ashland countryside—a two-story building that had probably been painted a bright, glossy red at one time but whose color had slowly faded to a dull, rusty brown. The double doors on the front were closed, and shades had been pulled down over the windows, but a faint, steady hum sounded in the distance. Probably a generator to power the lights and pump some heat into the barn.

The double doors were the only way in on the ground level that I could see, so I looked up at the second story, which featured a couple of windows, along with a large single door that probably led to a hayloft. No shades covered the glass on the second-story windows, and I didn't see anyone moving around up there.

Fletcher had always said it was better to come at your enemies from an unexpected angle, and the old man's words of wisdom were especially true in this case, when Owen was trapped inside the barn with who knew how many giants. So I started looking for a way to get up to the second level, and my gaze locked onto a drainpipe at one corner of the building. Perfect.

I didn't want to waste time turning my phone on, so I pulled the dead giant's phone out of my pocket and texted Sophia, telling her where I was and what was going on. I also sent the same message to Finn and Bria, even though I doubted they had switched their phones back on yet. Once that was done, I slid the device back into my pocket.

I looked around again, but the barn remained silent and shut up, so I surged to my feet, plowed my way through the overgrown field, crossed the mowed yard, and plastered myself up against the side of the building. I drew in quick, steady breaths through my nose, trying to listen above the roar of my heart, but no shouts sounded, and no one seemed to have spotted me.

I took hold of the drainpipe and gave it a hard, sharp tug to determine if it would hold my weight. The dull gray pipe looked as old and run-down as the rest of the barn, but it didn't budge, squeak, or protest, so I wrapped both hands around it and started climbing.

I dug my boots into the wood on either side of the drainpipe, using my feet to help support me as I reached higher and higher and shimmied up the pipe. The metal was so cold that it burned my hands, but I didn't dare use my Stone magic to harden my skin.

If an elemental was inside the barn, they might sense me using my magic and come outside to investigate. I didn't want that. Not until Owen was safe. Then I would take on anybody here who had an ounce of magic, along with everyone who didn't.

As an assassin, I'd done my fair share of spidery climbing, and it didn't take me long to reach the second level. One of the windows was right beside the drainpipe, so I grabbed hold of the wooden frame. I was only mildly surprised when it easily slid up. People thought that locking the doors and windows on the first floor was enough to keep out bad folks. And it usually was, but most folks weren't the Spider, and I was just about the baddest of them all.

I slid the window up as high as it would go, then grabbed the bottom of the frame with both hands, pulled myself forward, and slithered through the opening. I went headfirst, and I ended up sliding down into a loose mound of old, moldy hay. Ugh. The hay scratched my face and tickled my nose, and I had to swallow down a sneeze. I waited a moment, lying there, but no shouts or alarms sounded, so I slowly sat up.

I was in a hayloft, surrounded by, you guessed it, hay. Several bales were stacked up along the walls, while more loose hay covered the floor, including the spot where I was sitting. The inside of the barn looked just as decrepit as the outside, and several of the wooden floorboards were cracked or missing, while others sagged underneath the weight of the bales.

The only good thing about the loft was that it didn't look like anyone had been up there in ages, given the thick layer of dust that coated everything. Even more dust motes swirled through the air like mosquitoes, and I had to swallow down another sneeze.

I reached out and closed the open window behind me. Then I palmed a knife and slowly, carefully, quietly crawled out of the hay.

The loft was shaped like a giant U, with a set of stairs in the middle leading down to the ground. I crept over to the wooden railing that cordoned off the right side of the loft and peered down at the first floor.

I wasn't sure what I'd been expecting. Some old, forgotten farm equipment slowly rusting away. Maybe an old junker car with flat tires that had been stripped for parts and left to rot. Maybe even some barn cats sleeping in the dusty piles of hay.

What I didn't expect were the thick brown leather couches arranged around low tables full of laptops, monitors, keyboards, gaming consoles, and other high-tech computer equipment. A couple of refrigerators lined one of the walls, with cases of beer piled on top of them, along with bags of potato chips, pretzels, candy bars, and other snacks. Several bales of hay were also scattered around, with swords, daggers, spears, and other sharp, pointy, medieval weapons sticking out of them, as though the bales were oversize pincushions.

But the centerpiece of the first floor was a long, wide table covered with bright green felt that held an enormous diorama of a medieval landscape. Miniature gray stone castles, green paper mountains with painted white peaks, blue-tinted water in little rivers that snaked across the landscape, even dwarves, giants, sorcerers, and other metal figurines clutching small silver swords, shields, and magic wands. The diorama featured all that and more, and it was an impressive, museum-quality display.

Several cushioned chairs were spaced around the diorama, along with smaller tables covered with pens, notepads, and plastic containers filled with neon-colored, multi-sided dice. Still more tables bristled with bottles of paint, brushes, colored paper, and other art supplies.

This wasn't a barn—it was a ren-faire, role-playing, model-making gamer's paradise.

Definitely *not* what I had expected, and the jumble of items only made me more confused. Who owned all this stuff? And why keep it in a decrepit old barn? And what did any of this have to do with kidnapping Owen?

The low murmur of voices sounded down below, and a door creaked open somewhere in the back of the first floor, out of my line of sight. Then the distinctive *slap-slap-slap-slap* of boots against concrete rang out.

A few seconds later, Pirate Queen Celeste strolled into view. She was still wearing her red leather costume, along with her two ruby-studded swords, and that silver tiara still glinted on her head.

And she wasn't alone.

Four black-leather-clad giants followed her into the front part of the barn. Two of the men sat down next to each other and started typing on two separate laptops that were perched at one end of the diorama table. For a moment, I thought they were booting up some game, but rows of text and numbers filled their screens, not bright, flashy graphics. The other two giants lounged on one of the couches.

"Did anyone follow you?" Celeste asked. "Or try to stop you?"

One of the giants on the couch shook his head. "Nope. I waited until Grayson took a break from the forge, then bashed him upside the head just like you told me to. The boys helped me carry him through the park. We told everyone that he was drunk and played it for laughs, and they all thought it was part of the show. We walked right through the crowd, and no one batted an eye."

Celeste nodded her approval.

"What about Blanco?" another giant piped up.

Celeste shrugged. "Lancelot took care of her. We're free and clear."

I let out a quiet sigh of relief. Apparently, Celeste had believed my fake text claiming that Lancelot and his friends had eliminated me. Good. That at least gave me the small advantage of surprise.

"But it's a shame that Lancelot got to kill her instead of me. After all this work and training, I wanted to go a few rounds with the infamous Spider." Celeste stuck out her red lips in an exaggerated pout.

My hand tightened around my knife. She didn't realize it yet, but she was going to get her wish to tangle with me—and she was going to bleed out all over that concrete floor.

"All right, then," Celeste said. "Let's get on with it."

She turned to the giants on the couch and made a sharp, sweeping motion with her hand, as though she really was a queen telling her minions to scuttle away. The giants nodded, got to their feet, and disappeared into the back of the barn. A few seconds later, they reappeared, carrying a third man between them.

Owen.

7

The two giants half dragged, half carried Owen over to a wooden chair close to the diorama and threw him down into the seat.

An ugly bruise had bloomed like a purple pansy on the left side of Owen's face, and blood had oozed out of a deep, nasty cut in the center of the swelling, trickled down his cheek, and dried on his skin like rusty paint. Owen blinked and blinked, but he didn't resist as the giants tied his arms down to the chair with thick, heavy ropes. He was still clearly dazed from the hard hit he'd taken when the men attacked him behind the blacksmith forge.

Some of the tension in my chest eased, and my breath escaped in a relieved rush that sent the dust motes spinning through the air. Yes, Owen was injured, but Jo-Jo could use her Air magic to heal his head, along with all the other damage the giants had done. I just needed to get him out of the barn first—and figure out exactly who these people were and why they had kidnapped him.

I could understand Hugh Tucker, Mason, or some other Circle member snatching Owen to lure me into a trap, but it sounded like Lancelot had been ordered to kill me outright, while Owen was still alive. Why eliminate me and keep him alive? Unless . . .

Unless this was all about *Owen*.

This whole time, I'd thought someone had been using Owen to get to me. But these people didn't care about me at all, other than making sure that I stayed out of their way. No, they had been after Owen this whole time. But why?

I studied Celeste and the four giants, but I had never seen any of them before today. I was certain of it. I also didn't remember seeing their faces in the files Fletcher had kept on Ashland's many criminals. These were either low-level players or new folks in town. But that still didn't answer the question of why they had kidnapped Owen.

Celeste glanced over at the two giants in front of the laptops. "Aren't you ready yet?" she snapped, an impatient note in her voice. "How long does it take to type in a few passwords?"

"A few *dozen* passwords," one of the giants corrected her, still tapping keys the whole time. "And we're almost ready. We're just logging into all the accounts so that we can see the transactions and make sure that everything processes correctly."

My eyes narrowed. Accounts? Transactions?

The giant was making it sound like this was all about . . . *money*.

Kidnapping someone and cleaning out their personal and business holdings was a common enough scheme, especially in a place as corrupt and violent as Ashland, but I still wondered exactly *why* Celeste and the giants had chosen Owen out of all the businesspeople in the city.

It wasn't like they'd seen Owen walking down a dark street at midnight and decided to grab him on the spur of the moment. This whole setup reeked of weeks, if not months, of careful planning. But how had Celeste and her men even known that

Owen was going to be at the renaissance faire? It wasn't like he'd posted photos of his blacksmith costume on social media like his younger sister, Eva, would have. The only people who had known that Owen was going to be here were me and my friends and of course—

A faint, ominous *creak* sounded. I froze, as did Celeste and the giants on the first floor.

She yanked her two swords out of their scabbards and snapped them up. "What was that?"

The two giants who'd dragged Owen in here drew their own swords and started looking around, while the other two men in front of the computers stopped their staccato typing, their heads swiveling left and right, searching for the source of the noise.

A bad, bad feeling filled my stomach. I shifted my weight the tiniest bit to the right. Sure enough, another faint, ominous *creak* sounded.

I was the one making the telltale noise.

I grimaced and glanced down. For the first time, I noticed that the boards under my feet contained several deep, jagged cracks, far more cracks than the surrounding wood. My grimace deepened. I'd picked exactly the wrong spot to crouch down and spy on my enemies.

I slid my knife back up my sleeve, then slowly stood up and scooted one of my feet to the side. I was trying to get off the weakest-looking board, but the next one I stepped onto wasn't any better, and a third ominous *creak* rang out. I scooted my foot to a different board, and that *creak* cranked up into a low, steady whine.

I grimaced again and glanced around, trying to find a sturdier board to stand on, but there was nowhere for me to go. All the wood up here was cracked and rotten. So I changed tactics, leaning forward and stretching my hand out toward the window. Maybe I could at least grab hold of the windowsill and take some of my weight off the weak wood—

Too late.

Crack! Crack! Crack!

One after another, the boards splintered, and the entire floor gave way beneath my feet.

Apparently, I was the straw that broke the hayloft.

For a moment, I had the weightless sensation of falling, but then gravity set in, sucking me down, down, down. It all happened so fast that I didn't have time to grab hold of my Stone magic and harden my skin, but I landed on one of the bales that wasn't filled with weapons, and the hay softened my landing.

But smacking onto a solid surface was never pleasant, and pain spiked through my back. The blow also punched the breath out of my body, and I lay there sprawled across the hay bale and broken boards for several seconds, just trying to get air back down into my lungs.

While I sucked down breath after breath, two of the giants rushed forward and flanked me, their swords still clutched in their hands.

When I felt steady enough, I slowly sat up and dusted the splinters of wood and bits of hay off my clothes. Then I looked at the giants.

"Hey, fellas," I wheezed. "What's up?"

Celeste stepped forward, both of her swords still in her hands. She eyed me a moment, then jerked her head at the giants. "Get her up."

The two men holstered their weapons, stepped forward, and hauled me to my feet. One of them held me still while the other man patted me down. He found all five of my knives, which he tossed onto the top of the hay bale. Once that man had gotten rid of my knives, the other giant let go of my arm, and they both stepped back. Fools. They should have realized that I didn't need my blades to kill them.

I looked over at Owen. "You okay?"

He blinked away the rest of his daze and focused on me. "Just a little headache. You?" He nodded, and I realized that he was staring at my left arm.

"Oh, just a little slice with a sword. Nothing to worry about. You know I've had worse." I winked at him, and Owen grinned back at me.

"Well, if I were the two of you, I would be very worried right now," Celeste purred.

She started twirling her swords around in her hands, just as she had done earlier during the pirate show, and her hazel eyes started glowing with a bright, golden light. And just like at the pirate show, I sensed a faint gust of magic, one that slowly grew stronger and stronger the longer and faster Celeste spun her weapons around.

A sharp static charge filled the air, raising the hair on my arms and neck. In an instant, I felt like dozens of tiny invisible needles were stabbing into my skin over and over again, and I had to grind my teeth to keep from snarling. The uncomfortable pricking sensation reminded me of Jo-Jo's Air magic, but it wasn't quite the same.

It was *worse*.

Celeste was still twirling her swords around, but the blades seemed much brighter than before, almost as if they were . . . *glowing*. That bad, bad feeling filled my stomach again, and I peered at her weapons more closely.

Hot golden sparks of electricity popped, crackled, and sizzled up and down the two blades, streaking from the hilts to the points and back again in explosive waves. Most elementals were gifted in Air, Fire, Ice, or Stone, but Celeste's power was electricity, an offshoot of Air, just like Owen's metal magic was an offshoot of Stone. I grimaced again. Of course, she had electrical magic. Because she wasn't nearly dangerous enough with those swords already.

Celeste must have gotten tired of showing off, because she stopped spinning her swords around and slowly lowered the weapons to her sides, although those golden sparks kept dancing up and down the lengths of the blades.

"I can't believe you're an assassin, much less the Spider, the queen of the Ashland underworld." She sneered. "And to think that I used to be your biggest fan. I got into sword fighting because of you, and I even dressed up like you at the summer faire last year. What a fucking disappointment."

My fan? Training with swords? Dressing up like me? I'd expected threats of violence and promises of pain, torture, and death. Not . . . whatever this was.

"You're my fan? How do you even know who I am?"

Celeste arched an eyebrow. "Are you kidding? You're a real-life assassin who supposedly has a heart of gold and helps people who can't help themselves. Of course I know who you are. *Everyone* on the ren-faire circuit knows who you are. You're practically a fucking folk hero."

All four of the giants nodded, confirming her words, and a couple of them gave me sly, goofy grins. I glanced over at Owen, who looked as bewildered as I felt.

Celeste shook her head. "But I guess this just goes to show that the old saying is true and that you should never meet your idols, because they'll only end up disappointing you."

"And how have I disappointed you?"

She let out a loud, derisive snort. "Forgive me for not admiring someone stupid enough to fall through a rickety old hayloft."

She had a point, although I would never admit it. Plunging through the hayloft hadn't been one of my finest moments, but sometimes Lady Luck just screwed me over like that. What mattered was picking myself up again and getting back into the fight, and I was an expert at both of those things.

Unlike these people, who seemed to be . . . *amateurs*.

All the talk of being my fan and dressing up made me think that Celeste and her friends were only playing at being hardened criminals instead of being bona fide villains. I eyed the golden sparks of magic still shooting off her swords. Well, she wasn't playing. She definitely wanted to murder me in the most painful manner possible.

Had Owen and I really been captured by some weekend ren-faire players? I bit back a groan. Finn would *never* let me live this down—provided Owen and I made it out of here alive.

"Complete and utter disappointment," Celeste said for the third time.

Fan or not, I'd had enough of her snide criticism. She thought she was better than me? Well, we'd see about that.

"I bet Lancelot and his two friends were disappointed in me too—right up until I killed them."

My harsh words wiped the goofy grins off the giants' faces, although they didn't seem to faze Celeste.

"You guys don't know what you've gotten yourself into. This is real life, not some game you're playing on that diorama," I snarled. "You're right. I am the Spider, I am a real assassin, and I am really, truly going to *kill you all dead* unless you leave right now."

I turned my cold, wintry gray gaze to first one giant, then another. The two standing near me shifted nervously on their feet, but they didn't back away, while the other two in front of the laptops stayed in their seats. I'd given them a chance to save themselves, and they hadn't taken it. What happened next was on them.

Celeste snorted again. "Lancelot was an idiot who barely knew the sharp end of his sword from his ass. I won't make the same mistake. Trust me on that."

She spun her swords around again, putting even more flashy flourish into her smooth moves, along with another wave of bright, crackling electricity. Arrogant show-off.

Still, as much as I would have liked to charge across the barn, wrest one of those swords away from her, and bury the blade in her heart, I held my position. Celeste was close to Owen, and she could easily slice one of her swords across his throat before I could get to him.

I looked at Owen, who nodded back. He realized that I was going to have to wait for the right moment to strike, just like he was waiting.

I focused on Celeste again. When in doubt, start talking to stall for some more time. I hoped she wouldn't be too disappointed in me for using the oldest trick in the book.

"What do you want?" I asked. "Why did you kidnap Owen, and why did you order your goons to try to kill me? And why are you calling yourself the Black Rook?"

Celeste frowned a moment, as if she didn't know what I was talking about, but then her pretty face creased into a smug smile, and she let out a light, pealing laugh. The giants joined in with hearty chuckles. The mocking sounds grated on my nerves even more than the awful feel of her electrical magic did.

"What's so funny?" I growled.

"Oh, you dumb little Spider," Celeste purred, smiling even wider than before. "Whoever said that *I* was the Black Rook?"

Confusion filled me, but then I looked at her costume again. No black feathers adorned her red leather, and she wasn't wearing any sort of bird symbols. More confusion filled me. But if Celeste wasn't the Black Rook, then who was? And what did they want from Owen?

"Oh, Gin," a low voice called out. "I was actually hoping not to involve you in this, but you just wouldn't stay out of the way. Then again, I had heard that was one of your more annoying traits."

198 JENNIFER ESTEP

I didn't recognize the voice, but Owen jerked back in his chair as though he'd just been slapped across the face. His head whipped to the left, and I followed his gaze.

Footsteps sounded in the back of the barn, and a figure wearing a long, hooded black cloak stepped out from behind another stack of hay bales. This must be the mysterious Black Rook.

Owen's jaw clenched, and his eyes glittered with anger, but I still didn't understand what was going on. Who was this person?

The Black Rook stopped in an open space near the middle of the barn and pushed back the hood of his cloak, revealing a very familiar face.

Darrell Kline.

8

Darrell had drastically changed since the last time I'd seen him during the pirate show.

His green velvet derring-do Robin Hood costume had vanished, along with his silver glasses and clipboard, and he was now wearing a far more badass ensemble of a black leather shirt, pants, and boots. Soft, glossy black feathers trimmed his black cloak, adding to his dark, ominous look. A large silver pin shaped like a cawing bird with ruby eyes hooked the front of the cloak together just below his throat. Not just any bird, I realized.

A rook.

"*You're* the Black Rook?" I asked.

He lifted his chin and gave me a cold, razor-thin smile. His clothes weren't the only thing that had changed—so had Darrell himself.

Gone was the nice, polite accountant who volunteered at the faire, and in his place was a much harder, more confident man. His body seemed bigger and stronger, his hazel eyes were brighter, and even his previously shaggy sandy-brown hair had been slicked back into a smoother, more menacing style. I felt like I'd just seen a snake shed its skin, and I got the impression that I was finally seeing the true Darrell Kline, or Black Rook, or whatever he was calling himself.

Darrell held his hands out wide, preening and showing off his costume. "Well, I imagine my outfit gave it away, but yes, Gin. *I* am the Black Rook. Just like you're the assassin the Spider. Only today, you got caught in my web. Ha-ha-ha-ha."

I rolled my eyes at his bad pun, but Darrell ignored me and turned to Celeste, who came over, leaned forward, and pressed a loud, smacking kiss to his lips. Darrell grinned and slipped an arm around her waist, careful of her two swords as he hugged her close. Celeste let out a little giggle and kissed him again before stepping away.

So not only did Celeste work for Darrell, but the two of them were involved as well, like an evil, ren-faire Maid Marian and Robin Hood come to life. Terrific. Just terrific. As if this wasn't weird enough already.

Darrell reached into his pants pocket. I tensed, thinking that he was grabbing a dagger or some other weapon, but he only pulled out his phone and started swiping through screens.

"I thought volunteers were supposed to turn off their phones," I sniped. "In order to add to the magical *atmosphere*."

Darrell shrugged. "Normally, I would do that, but you can't steal millions of dollars just by brandishing a sword at someone. These days, you need computers for that sort of thing."

Owen glanced over at the two giants still typing on their laptops, then focused on Darrell again. Owen's violet eyes narrowed in understanding.

"This is about the Harrison account, isn't it?" he accused. "I knew there was something wrong with the numbers. I *knew* it."

Darrell shrugged again. "Of course there's something wrong with the numbers. I've been cooking the books and siphoning money from that account and a few others for months now. Five thousand here, ten thousand there. Not too much at one time, but it started to add up. I was hoping to get a few more weeks and paydays out of the accounts before slipping quietly off into the night, but then you announced that you were bringing in that outside forensic accountant to go over everything on Monday."

He shook his head as though he was deeply disappointed in Owen's thoroughness. "I knew the game was up, but instead of taking a few more thousand dollars and disappearing, I decided to double down and go for one last big score. Besides, why just steal from a few measly accounts when I can clean out everything you have? *All* the accounts, *all* at once."

"You bastard," Owen growled. "You're nothing but a damn thief."

Despite his harsh tone and fierce words, worry still filled his face. Owen was a successful businessman with stakes in mining, lumber, and other operations in Ashland and beyond, and he had access to accounts and assets that were worth millions of dollars. If Darrell stole all that money . . . Well, bankruptcy wouldn't be the worst part of it. Owen's reputation would be ruined, and a lot of people who worked with him or for him could also lose everything.

"Why?" Owen asked the inevitable question. "Why are you doing this? Why are you stealing from me?"

"It's been obvious for quite some time that I'd gone as high in your company as I could and that I was never going to get out of middle management." Darrell stabbed his finger at me, as if that was my fault. "Something that became crystal clear after you and Gin hooked up. You started taking more and more of your business to Finnegan fucking Lane and asking *his* advice about various accounts and investments instead of *mine*."

So this was all about money. It usually was in Ashland.

Something that Owen had said in Jo-Jo's salon this morning popped into my mind. "Wait a second. You were at that charity auction a few weeks ago, weren't you? Owen said he didn't even remember bidding on the faire tickets. That's because he *never* bid on them. *You* did. You just needed Owen to supposedly win the tickets in order to get him here."

Darrell grinned, as though he was pleased that I'd figured out his scheme. "Exactly! I needed to get Owen out of his comfort zone and into mine. Of course, I expected him to bring Eva today—not you, Finnegan Lane, and your sister the detective. But I knew that my plan would still work. I just had to get you out of the way first."

So that was why he'd posted the giants outside the Pork Pit food truck: to keep me busy and stop me from interfering while the rest of his men kidnapped Owen.

"I wasn't paying and promoting you enough, so you decided to steal from me?" Owen growled again.

Instead of answering Owen's accusation, Darrell shifted on his feet and adjusted the silver rook pin at his throat. I focused on the bird's ruby eyes and reached out with my Stone magic. The rubies were whispering about how pretty and expensive they were, just like the jewels embedded in the hilts of Celeste's swords still were. Their outfits had both cost a pretty penny too, as had all the fancy gaming equipment and the diorama.

"You're broke," I said. "That's why you're really doing this."

Owen frowned. "What do you mean?"

I held my hands out wide. "Look at this place. All the monitors and gaming equipment, all the paint and art supplies for the diorama. None of that stuff is cheap. Neither are their costumes and weapons."

I snapped my fingers, remembering something else. "And Darrell has even more of this stuff at home. He showed me pictures of his collectibles during the holiday party at the Pork Pit."

Darrell didn't respond, but a pink flush crept up his neck, his lips pinched together into a tight, thin line, and he crossed his arms over his chest in a defensive motion. Guilty as charged.

"Gin's right. You're doing this because you're a greedy

bastard, not because I hurt your feelings." Owen shook his head. "And here I thought you actually believed in all this medieval, ren-faire stuff about duty and honor and loyalty."

"Oh, I do believe in it, but my favorite characters to play have always been the rogues, the thieves, the pirates." Darrell tipped his head to me. "And especially the assassins who take what they want and kill whomever they like."

"Gin has more honor and loyalty in her pinkie than you will ever have," Owen snarled.

Darrell gave him an amused look. "Aw, how noble of you to defend your lady's honor. I hope Gin appreciates the gesture, especially since it's the last thing you'll ever do for her."

He slid his phone back into his pocket, then walked over to the two giants still sitting at the computers. "Are we ready to transfer the money?"

One of the giants flashed him a thumbs-up and handed him a tablet. Darrell clutched the device in the crook of his elbow, then strolled back over to Owen.

"And now, boss, it's time to give me access to your accounts—all of them." Darrell loomed over him. "I need your master login and password, as well as your personal authentication keywords."

"Fuck off," Owen snarled. "I'm not giving you a thing—not one damn thing."

"I thought you might say that."

Darrell stepped back and jerked his head at Celeste, who twirled her swords around in her hands again. I knew what she was going to do, and I took a step forward to try to stop her, but the two giants raised their fists and cracked their knuckles in warning. They were standing between me and Owen, as were Darrell and Celeste, and any one of them could easily kill Owen before I could get to him. So as much as I hated it, I stopped, gritted my teeth, and held up my hands, surrendering to the bastards.

For now.

Celeste made sure that I wasn't going to interfere, then whipped around and slammed the hilt of her first sword straight into Owen's face.

Crunch.

The sound of his nose breaking seemed as loud as a clap of thunder in the barn. Owen let out a low groan of pain, and blood gushed down his face.

Celeste hummed with happiness. And then she hit him again. And then again and then again.

She slammed the hilts of her swords into Owen's face, chest, and arms over and over, like he was a dummy she was practicing her moves on. Each pain-filled grunt that escaped his lips was like a punch to my own heart. Celeste also put a bit of her electrical magic into the blows, making Owen's entire body twitch and jerk and his skin blister and burn.

The acrid stench of his singed flesh was one of the worst things I had ever smelled in my entire life.

Through it all, Owen stared at me, his violet gaze steady on mine. The absolute love and trust shining in his eyes made my own heart squeeze tight in response. Despite our dire situation, he still believed that I would get us out of this. That I would save us. His unwavering trust filled me with a warm rush of love, along with an iron determination not to let him down.

But Celeste could still slit Owen's throat before I could reach him, so I had to stand there and watch while the bitch tortured him.

After a few minutes, Celeste finally lowered her weapons and stepped back. Owen coughed and coughed, trying to get his breath back after all the brutal blows, and his arms and legs kept twitching from the lingering stings of her electricity. After the better part of a minute, he finally stopped coughing, although the faint hitch and wheeze in his breath indicated that he probably had at least one cracked or broken rib, if not more.

Celeste smirked at me. My hands clenched into tight fists. She was going to die for hurting him—she just didn't realize it yet.

Darrell gestured at his partner in crime. "I like to play the part of a thief, but Celeste here, well, she's more of a barbarian at heart. I love that about her."

He gave an elaborate hand flourish and bowed low to her, as though he really was a gallant knight and she was some fair maiden, instead of them both being rotten and treacherous to the core. Darrell straightened back up, and Celeste blew him an air kiss, which he caught and dramatically pressed to his heart. Ugh. *Kill me now*, just like Finn had said.

Owen looked up at the two of them. Then he leaned forward and spat out a mouthful of blood right onto Darrell's shiny black boots. I grinned. And that was one of the reasons I loved him.

"How's that for barbaric?" Owen rasped.

Darrell's nose crinkled with disgust. Celeste stepped forward and hit Owen again, making him cough up more blood. Worry twisted my chest, but I didn't move. I couldn't risk attacking while Celeste and her swords were still that close to Owen.

Darrell eyed his former boss a moment longer, then smiled, as if some new, horrible thought had occurred to him.

"Well, if you won't give up the information to save yourself, then maybe you'll give it up to save your own precious assassin queen." Darrell jerked his head at Celeste, who grinned and stalked over to me.

She gestured at the two giants, who stepped forward and latched onto my arms. I didn't resist, even though I knew how much this was going to hurt.

Celeste moved so that she was standing right in front of me, still clutching her two swords. Her lips puckered as she studied me, clearly thinking about where and how badly to hurt me. She tilted her head to the side, then snapped her hand forward and slammed her sword hilt into my face, just like she'd done to Owen.

Pain erupted in my left cheek and quickly radiated out through my skull like a string of grenades exploding one after another. I staggered back, and I would have fallen on my ass if the giants hadn't been holding on to me. Even then, I listed around like a ship on a stormy sea, and more than a few white stars winked on and off in my field of vision.

"Wait!" Owen yelled. "Stop!"

But Celeste didn't stop. Instead, she lashed out with one of her blades, opening up a gash along my left bicep. The deep cut was bad enough, but she also put some of her electricity into the blow, and the stinging jolts blasted over me like I'd just touched a live wire.

Sweat popped out on my forehead, my teeth rattled together, and I accidentally bit my own tongue, adding to my misery. My body involuntarily jerked and flailed, but the giants held me fast until the electricity faded away. Somehow I swallowed down a scream of pain, even though I felt like my left arm was on fire.

Celeste smirked and drew her sword back for another strike, but Darrell held out his hand, stopping her.

"I think that's enough for now. Let's see if hurting Gin has made Owen more cooperative." He turned to the other man. "Well, Owen? What do you say? Do you feel like giving up those passwords now?"

Owen glared at his former accountant, his violet eyes practically glowing with fury. "I'm going to kill you for hurting Gin," he growled.

Darrell laughed. "Oh, I doubt that. As soon as I have your money, Celeste and I are leaving Ashland for good. In a few hours, we'll be on a Caribbean island, shopping for yachts and whatever else strikes our fancy, and drinking and spending all our cares away. Isn't that right, my queen?"

Celeste beamed at him. "Absolutely."

Shopping for yachts? Well, someone was taking their pirate fantasy a little too far, but I hoped they enjoyed it—because it was going to be the last thing they ever enjoyed.

Darrell went back over to Owen and bent down, waggling his tablet in Owen's face. "The passwords. Or Celeste goes back to practicing her sword and magic skills on Gin."

Owen looked at me, then at my two giant guards, then at Celeste, who was still standing in front of me with her swords clutched in her hands. Finally, he focused on me again.

Worry, fear, and concern tightened his face, but they weren't nearly as strong as the other two emotions burning in his violet gaze: his love for me and his determination that we were both getting out of this alive.

I nodded, telling him that I was ready to move. "It's all right, Owen. Just give him the passwords."

"Yes, Owen," Darrell sneered. "Give me the passwords. *Now.* Or your precious Gin dies."

Celeste stepped closer to me and lifted one of her swords, resting the sharp blade up against my throat. She smirked, then pressed the edge into my neck, nicking my skin and drawing a bit of blood. She was going to slit my throat the second Darrell had what he needed from Owen. Well, let her try. She was the one who wouldn't be getting out of here alive.

Darrell glanced over at the two giants in front of the computers. This time, they both flashed him a thumbs-up, telling him they were ready to rock 'n' roll and steal everything from Owen. He nodded, then turned back to Owen.

"Give me your master password," Darrell demanded.

Owen wet his lips, but he didn't say anything.

Darrell sighed, then lifted his arm and backhanded Owen. The sharp *crack* of the blow echoed through the barn, further hardening my resolve.

Owen bent over double, coughing and coughing. That went

on for several seconds before he finally got his breath back and straightened up.

"The password," Darrell demanded again. "This is your last chance. Otherwise, Celeste starts cutting off pieces of Gin."

Owen mumbled something unintelligible.

Darrell frowned and leaned down. "What? What did you say?"

Owen mumbled again. This time, everyone looked at him, including Celeste, who shifted on her feet and lowered her sword one precious inch away from my throat. Amateurs. They should have known better than to take their eyes off me.

"What did you say?" Darrell asked again.

Owen lifted his head and smiled. "I said I'm going to enjoy watching you die, you backstabbing son of a bitch."

Before Darrell could move or react, Owen snapped his head forward.

Crunch.

This time, Darrell's nose was the one that broke. He screamed and stumbled away, blood gushing down his face and his tablet slipping from his hand. He sucked down a breath, probably to order Celeste to cut my throat, but Owen let out a loud roar and surged to his feet, even though his arms were still tied down to the chair. He ran forward and smashed his body—chair and all—straight into Darrell.

And that's when the real ren-faire battle began.

9

Owen and Darrell crashed to the floor with a loud, thunderous roar.

The wooden chair must have been as rickety as the hayloft boards, because it splintered to pieces under Owen's weight. He rolled over and up onto his knees, then ripped the ropes off his arms. The second he was free, Owen threw himself on top of Darrell and started punching him.

Celeste cursed and started in that direction to help Darrell, but I kicked out and drove my foot into the back of her left thigh. She let out a loud, surprised shriek and tumbled to ground, although she managed to hang on to her swords.

Those two giants were still holding on to me, so I turned to the one on my right and drove my foot into the side of his ankle, which let out a loud, sickening *pop!* The giant screamed and loosened his grip. I shoved my hand down between us and grabbed the silver sword out of the scabbard on his belt. It was heavy, just like all the giants' weapons were, but I managed to slice it across his stomach, and he dropped to the ground, screaming and clutching at the wound.

I turned toward the second giant, who was still hanging on

to me, his mouth gaping open in shock. I yanked my arm free of his grip, wrapped both hands around the hilt of my stolen sword, and sliced it across his chest. He too screamed and fell to the ground.

The two giants might be out of the fight, but Celeste was definitely not.

She surged back to her feet and whirled around to me. She was still clutching her swords, and golden sparks of electricity started sizzling up and down the blades again. I reached for my own Stone magic, using it to harden my skin, although Celeste didn't seem to notice.

"I'm going to cut you to pieces for that!" she hissed.

"Do your worst!" I hissed right back at her.

Celeste let out a shriek of rage and charged forward. I also screamed with rage and stepped up to meet her.

Celeste whirled and twirled her swords every which way, slicing out with them over and over again. I might be skilled with my knives, but it was all I could do to lift the giant's heavy sword and block her vicious blows. Yep, I definitely needed to add medieval weapons to my training regimen. Some heavier weights too.

After a particularly fast, vigorous exchange, Celeste managed to knock my stolen sword out of my hand. The weapon sailed away and landed point-down in one of the hay bales. Ah, the irony. I couldn't have done that if I'd tried a hundred times.

Celeste tightened her grip on her swords and reached for even more of her magic, so that the blades seemed to be made of golden electricity instead of metal. "Now there's nothing to keep me from slicing you to ribbons and then frying your weak, clumsy ass."

She let out a loud yell and charged forward, slashing her swords through the air as fast as she could. I spun out of the way of her first attack, then her second one, but I couldn't avoid her third strike, and she sliced one of her swords across the back of my thigh.

The hard, bruising blow made me stumble, but thanks to my Stone magic, the blade didn't actually bite into my flesh, and her electricity only scorched my costume, not my skin. Still, I let out a loud, agonized scream, flailed around, and dropped to one knee, as though I was severely injured.

Celeste thought she'd won, and she started circling me, still clutching her swords. Electrical sparks fell off the blades like acid raindrops and crackled against the floor. I felt like I was trapped in a fireworks show, although I maintained my grip on my Stone magic to protect my skin from her hot, burning power.

She was savoring the moment. Well, I hoped she enjoyed it. Because I was a long way from done, something she was going to realize in another minute, two tops.

"I don't see why Darrell was so worried about you," she said. "Sure, you're a good fighter, but I'm better, especially with my swords. And my electricity gives me a clear advantage."

I could have told her that the better fighter didn't always win and that I'd killed a whole lot of people who'd been stronger than me in their magic, but I didn't waste my breath. She was already dead. She just didn't know it yet.

Instead, I looked past Celeste at Owen, who was still pummeling Darrell. The two giants who'd been sitting in front of the computers finally realized that their boss was going to lose the fight, and they surged to their feet and headed in that direction. Owen saw them coming, picked up one of the broken pieces of his chair, and threw it at them. Even though it was just a harmless piece of wood, the two giants still lurched back out of the way.

Celeste finally noticed that Owen was beating the shit out of her boyfriend, but instead of going over to help him, she turned back to me instead.

"Time to die, little Spider," she snarled.

She lifted one of her swords and then snapped it down. I didn't even try to avoid the blow. Instead, I reached for even more of my Stone magic, closed my hand into a fist, and smashed it up against her weapon.

CLANG!

Celeste wasn't expecting the concrete resistance of my Stone-hardened fist, and she lost her grip on her sword, which sailed through the air before landing point-down in that same hay bale right next to my weapon. Bull's-eye for a second time. Even Robin Hood would have been impressed with my aim today.

Surprise flickered in Celeste's hazel eyes, and she lashed out with her other sword, trying to drive it into my heart. This time, I reached out, wrapped my fingers around the blade, and used it like a lever to pull myself back up and onto my feet. Celeste snarled, gripped the hilt with both hands, and tried to wrest her sword free, but my Stone magic gave me a cement grip that she just couldn't break.

I dropped my free hand down by my side, this time reaching for my Ice magic. In an instant, I had formed a long, jagged Ice knife.

Celeste tried one last time to wrest her sword away, but I tightened my grip on the blade and yanked, pulling her toward me. Celeste growled and raised one of her hands to blast me in the face with her electricity, but I was quicker. I snapped up the Ice knife in my other hand and buried the cold shard in the side of her neck.

Her eyes bulged, and the golden glow of her electrical magic snuffed out of her gaze like a fire doused by a wet blanket. I twisted the cold shard in even deeper, staring at her the whole time.

"If you were a true fan, then you would know that no one does my job better than me," I hissed.

Celeste let out a strangled scream, almost as if she was agreeing with me. Then her eyes rolled up in the back of her head, and she crumpled to the ground with my Ice knife still stuck in her neck. Blood started pooling under her body. The scarlet sheen matched her fancy costume.

The pirate queen was dead.

"Celeste!" Darrell shouted. "No!"

He had finally managed to scramble away from Owen, who was now battling the two giants. Owen had gotten his hands on someone's sword, and one of the giants already lay dead at his feet. Owen snarled and engaged the second giant, swinging his stolen sword like it was his more familiar blacksmith hammer.

"Celeste!" Darrell shouted again. "Celeste!"

He raced in my direction. I reached for my Ice magic again, but before I could make another knife, he plowed into me. My legs hit something, and Darrell bent me backward. An instant later, my head snapped back against a hard surface, making me lose my grip on my Stone magic. White stars flashed in front of my eyes, and my skin reverted to its normal vulnerable texture.

It took me a moment to realize that I was now sprawled across the table with the fancy medieval diorama. Judging from the hard lumps poking into my back, I'd just flattened a couple of mountains and several legions of dwarves and giants.

I tried to rise, but Darrell shoved me right back down again, then grabbed one of the gray stone castles off the table.

"You bitch!" he screamed, his voice teetering on a plaintive wail. "You killed Celeste! You killed my pirate queen!"

He snapped the castle down, aiming for my nose, but I managed to catch his wrist in my hand and stop him from hitting me. But that was only part of the problem. The castle also featured a flag pole with a very long, very sharp point. Darrell snarled and pressed down, trying to drive the needlelike tip into my right eye.

My head was still spinning, and I was having trouble grabbing hold of my magic so I could blast him with my Ice power. He might be an amateur, but he could still kill me if he hit me in just the right spot—

Something silver glinted behind Darrell, who suddenly screamed and arched back. The miniature castle slipped from his hand, hit the side of the table, and bounced off, dropping to the floor. A hand grabbed Darrell's shoulder, yanking him away from me.

Owen was here.

I rolled off the table, landing hard on my knees on the floor. The fall rattled my brain again, making a few more white stars wink on and off in front of my eyes. I forced myself to scoot away from Darrell, but I didn't have to worry about him any longer.

Owen spun Darrell around, then stepped up and rammed his sword into the other man's stomach.

Darrell screamed again and clutched at Owen's costume, his face white with shock and pain.

"That's for hurting Gin," Owen growled. "And this is for hurting me."

He shoved the sword in even deeper, then yanked it out and pushed the other man away.

Darrell screamed again and stumbled back against the table hard enough to jostle the remaining castles, mountains, and figurines on the diorama. Het let out another strangled cry, then his legs went out from under him, and he sank to the floor. He tried to clamp his hands down over the wound, but he didn't have the strength for it, and he slowly pitched over onto his side.

Darrell landed right next to that gray stone castle he'd tried to stab into my face, and he lifted his arm, as though he was going to reach for it. But he was even weaker than before, and his hand flopped to the floor well short of the castle. He didn't move after that.

The Black Rook was dead.

Owen stood over Darrell, wheezing for breath and still clutching his stolen sword. He kicked Darrell in the ribs to make sure he was dead, then staggered over and dropped to his knees beside me.

"Gin! Are you okay?"

I blinked the last few stars out of my eyes and focused on him. Owen's face was a mess of cuts, blood, and bruises from fighting Darrell, and his broken nose had swelled up to almost twice its normal size, but he was as handsome as ever to me.

Owen leaned forward and cupped my cheek with his bloody hand, gently stroking his thumb across my skin. "Gin? Are you okay?" he repeated.

I reached up and grabbed his hand, squeezing it in my equally bloody one. "I'm okay. Thanks to you."

Owen grinned, his eyes glowing like beautiful violet moons. His grin widened, and he leaned down to kiss me—

The main barn doors burst open, and Finn, Bria, and Sophia charged inside. Finn and Bria were both clutching swords, while Sophia was holding her silver cutlass.

My friends skidded to a stop, their heads snapping from side to side as they took in the four dead giants, along with Celeste and Darrell and the fantasy diorama I'd flattened during the fight.

"Aw, man," Finn said, lowering his sword to his side. "We missed it! I totally wanted to engage in an old-fashioned sword duel!"

Sophia sighed with regret. "Me too."

I glanced at Celeste, who was lying on the floor a few feet away. She was still clutching one of her swords, and the blade gleamed with a bright, eerie light, as though it was going to start crackling with electricity again, even though she was dead.

I shuddered at the memory of her hot magic jolting through me. "Trust me. It's not as much fun as you'd think it would be."

"Are you guys okay?" Bria asked. "And who are these people, and why did they kidnap Owen?"

She came over and helped me to my feet, while Finn did the same for Owen.

"I'll tell you all about it," I answered my sister. "After we get out of here. I've had enough swords, pirate queens, and ren-faire goons to last me a lifetime."

"Me too," Owen murmured. "Me too."

I held out my hand, and Owen stepped forward and put his arm around me. Still holding on to each other, the two of us limped out of the barn.

✶ 10 ✶

Since we didn't want to ruin the rest of the ren faire for everyone else, Sophia agreed to dispose of the bodies in the barn, as well as the three giants I'd killed in the woods earlier. Finn stayed behind to help her, while Bria drove Owen and me over to Jo-Jo's salon.

We had to wait until Jo-Jo finished with her latest round of clients, but the dwarf healed Owen and me with her Air magic and sent us on our way. We ended up back at my house late that afternoon.

Owen was in the den, talking on the phone to Stuart Mosley at First Trust bank and trying to figure out just how much money Darrell had stolen and if he could get any of it back. While he hashed things out with Stuart, I went into the kitchen to make dinner.

Last night, I'd brought home some of the faire food that Sophia and I had prepared, and I quickly reheated the pulled chicken in some of Fletcher's barbecue sauce.

While the chicken was warming up, I microwaved a couple of potatoes until they were almost done, then sliced them in half and scooped out most of the insides. I combined the potato innards with sharp cheddar cheese, sour cream, green onions, and crumbled pieces of crispy applewood-smoked bacon. Then I refilled the potato boats with the mixture, sprinkled them with even more cheese, and slid them into the oven to finish baking.

After everything that had happened today, I wanted some warm comfort food, and barbecue chicken and twice-baked potatoes seemed like a good place to start.

I also sliced, buttered, and toasted some of Sophia's sourdough rolls in the oven and threw together a green salad filled with cherry tomatoes, carrots, and red onions and topped with a creamy blue-cheese dressing.

I had just finished putting everything on the kitchen table, along with a pitcher of raspberry lemonade, when Owen came in, sat down, and set his phone aside. I sat down with him, and we both tucked into our food.

The sweet and spicy barbecue chicken. Potatoes loaded with cheese and bacon. The warm toasted rolls. The crunchy, crispy salad with its blue-cheese tang. The fruity tartness of the lemonade. It was a delicious combination of flavors, aromas, and textures, and I enjoyed every single bite. Owen did too, judging by the fact that he went back for seconds, just like I did.

We didn't talk much during the meal, just enjoying the food, each other's company, and the fact that we had both survived another dangerous situation that we probably shouldn't have.

"What did Stuart say?" I asked after we'd taken the edge off our hunger.

"He agreed to let me access Darrell's accounts on Monday so I can recover some of the money he stole." Owen sighed and set his fork down. "There's not much left of it, though. Only a few thousand in his checking account. You were right about him spending it all. I'll have to cover most of the difference out of my own pocket."

"No, you won't."

He frowned. "What? Why not?"

I jerked my head over at one of the kitchen counters. "Because Sophia stopped by while you were talking to Stuart, and she brought you some presents."

Owen followed my gaze. Celeste's swords were sitting on the counter, along with the rook pin that Darrell had been wearing on his cloak.

"How is that going to help?" Owen asked.

"The rubies in the swords and the pin are worth quite a bit. We can go to Darrell's house tomorrow, break in, and loot the rest of his stuff. It shouldn't be too hard to find some buyers for his collectibles. I've already got Finn working on it. He's pitching it as an estate sale, and he'll run everything through First Trust. I don't know that we'll get all your money back, but we should be able to recover a good chunk of it."

Some of the tension eased out of Owen's shoulders, and a smile spread across his face. "Have I told you lately how much I love you?"

"Not nearly enough," I teased. "You know, a girl does like to hear those things from time to time."

His smile widened. "Well, I'll be sure to mention it more often, then. At the very least, every time you save me from ren-faire assassins."

My heart squeezed tight at how close I'd come to losing him to the Black Rook and Pirate Queen Celeste, but I winked, not wanting to ruin the lighthearted mood. "I'll hold you to that. And there is something else you could do for me."

"Name it."

I stabbed my finger at Celeste's swords. "Make me a pair of those. Just in case we ever do run into more ren-faire assassins. You never know in Ashland."

Owen nodded, and his eyes narrowed, as if he was already mentally designing the weapons. "Two silverstone swords. With long, sharp, plain blades. And some sapphires fitted together in the hilts to form your spider runes."

I could already see the weapons in my mind, and I knew they would be just as exquisite as the knives Owen had made for me. I grinned. "You certainly know the way to this assassin's heart."

For dessert, we had warm oatmeal-cherry crumble topped with vanilla-bean ice cream and drizzled with my homemade chocolate sauce. After we finished, Owen cleared the table while I lit a fire in the den. Then we curled up on the couch together, our arms wrapped around each other, staring into the bright, cheery flames and lost in our own thoughts.

"Do you want to talk about it?" I finally asked. "About Darrell? I know the two of you weren't all that close, but what he did still had to hurt."

A betrayal by someone you knew and considered a friend always left a far deeper mark than a random attack by a stranger.

"I liked Darrell. He was always nice, polite, and friendly, and I thought he was good at his job. I just didn't realize that he was a little *too* good at it." Owen grimaced. "I still can't believe he was plotting behind my back this whole time. And not just to steal money but to kidnap and kill me."

He fell silent, still staring into the flames. Several seconds passed before he spoke again.

"I guess it just goes to show that you don't really know some people the way you think you do. Maybe the ren faire should have a new theme next year. Maybe instead of *Winter's Web*, the organizers should call it *The Ides of Winter*." He let out a low, bitter laugh. "Hey, maybe I'll even dress up like Julius Caesar next year. After all, I've been betrayed, just like he was."

I kept quiet, sensing there was more he needed to say.

"And I can't help but feel stupid that I fell into Darrell's trap. I should have known something weird was going on when I supposedly won the faire tickets." He shook his head. "And I can't help but think that I could have done things differently. That if I'd just known how unhappy Darrell was, I could have done something to help him." His voice dropped. "Instead of killing him."

I sat up and looked at him. "It is *not* your fault that Darrell did what he did. People make their own choices, and they are responsible for their own actions and the consequences that come along with them. Darrell could have come to you and told you he'd made a mistake embezzling the money, and you would have helped him. I *know* you would have, because that's the kind of good, decent, honorable man you are. But Darrell was arrogant and stupid and greedy, and he decided to take what he wanted no matter how many people he had to hurt. That was his biggest mistake, and it ended up costing him everything."

Owen nodded, and some of the tension eased out of his body. "How did I ever get so lucky as to have you in my life?"

I grinned. "I could say the same thing about me having you."

He leaned over and kissed me. The brief brush of his lips against mine sent warmth shooting through my body and ignited a spark of desire deep in my stomach.

I drew back, then grinned again and clasped my hands to my heart. "Oh, my dear, sweet, humble blacksmith!" I cooed in a high, falsetto voice. "Oh, how you make me *swoon!*"

I put my hand up to my forehead, let out a long, loud, dramatic sigh, and then flopped back against the couch cushions, as though I was a genteel lady overcome with a case of the vapors.

Owen laughed and then bent forward at the waist, as though

he was taking a bow. "Why, thank you, fair lady. This humble blacksmith always aims to please his pirate queen assassin."

I crooked my finger at him. "Then come here and prove it," I murmured in a low, husky voice.

Owen grinned, leaned forward, and lowered himself on top of me so that we were both stretched out on the couch. I threaded my hands through his silky black hair and pulled his head down to mine. Our lips met, and I swiped my tongue against his. He deepened the kiss, plunging his tongue into my mouth. More sparks exploded in my stomach, and I sighed with happiness, wrapped my arms around his neck, and pulled him closer.

Owen kissed his way across my cheek, then sucked on the side of my neck. I drew in a breath, drawing his rich metallic scent deep into my lungs. He kept kissing my neck, even as his hands slid up my shirt. I wasn't wearing a bra, and he cupped my breasts, gently tweaking my nipples with his thumbs. Those sparks burned even brighter and coalesced into a liquid heat that flooded my entire body.

"You are wearing entirely too many clothes," Owen rumbled, still kneading my breasts.

"I was just thinking the same thing about you," I murmured back, running my hands down his strong, muscled back.

"Then let's fix that."

Owen grabbed me around the waist and sat up, pulling me up along with him. I lifted my arms over my head, and he stripped off my shirt, exposing my bare breasts.

His violet gaze darkened with desire. "Now, that's more like it."

He dipped his head to my right breast and gently caught my nipple between his teeth. Then he sucked on it hard before doing the same thing to my other breast. I gasped with pleasure and arched back to give him better access.

Owen kept sucking, licking, and kissing my breasts. That

liquid heat in my body burned a little hotter with every sure stroke of his fingers and every sly slide of his tongue. I reached down to get rid of his shirt the way he'd gotten rid of mine, but Owen caught my hand in his and pressed a kiss to my knuckles.

"Not yet," he murmured. "This blacksmith wants to thoroughly pleasure his lady first."

He gave me a wicked grin, then laid me back down on the couch and undid my jeans. I lifted my hips, and Owen slid the jeans off me, along with my underwear and socks. I lay there and watched while he got rid of his own clothes, then grabbed a condom from his wallet. I took my little white pills, but we always used extra protection.

The crackling flames bathed Owen in a soft glow, outlining his broad shoulders, his strong biceps, his muscled chest, and his long, hard erection. I let out a low wolf whistle of appreciation.

"Not so humble after all," I purred.

Owen winked. "Like I said before, I aim to please."

He got down on his knees beside the couch. He smoothed his hands down my thighs and eased them apart. My breath caught in my throat. I knew what was coming next and just how good it would be.

Owen gave me another wicked grin, then bent forward and put his mouth on me, sucking, licking, and kissing just as he'd done to my breasts. I moaned with pleasure and rocked forward, and he plunged his tongue even deeper inside me.

That liquid heat in my veins flared up into something hotter and far more intense, the pressure and the pleasure built and built, and it wasn't long before I cried out and exploded.

Owen kept right on sucking, licking, and kissing as the orgasm ripped through me, trying to bring me as much pleasure as possible. Finally, when my body had stilled, he lifted his head and looked at me.

"Is my lady pleased?" he murmured.

"Exceptionally. Now, come here, you," I growled.

I grabbed his hand and pulled him toward me. Owen laughed and climbed back onto the couch with me. Our mouths locked together, our tongues dueled back and forth, and our caresses became quicker, harder, and more intense.

Eventually, I flipped him over and teased his long, hard length with my tongue and mouth the same way he had teased me, trying to bring him as much pleasure as he had given me, as though this was the first time we'd been together instead of the hundredth. But in some ways, every time with Owen felt like the first time, and I always loved exploring all the hard, muscled planes of his body, from the scar that cut across his chin to his broad shoulders and all the way down his chest.

When Owen was ready, he covered himself with the condom, then picked me up and settled me on his lap. I looked into his eyes, then rocked forward, taking him deep inside me with one smooth motion. We both groaned, and he held on to my hips, urging me on as I surged forward time and time again, taking him deeper and deeper inside me, until we both reached the very peak of our pleasure and plunged over the edge together.

The humble blacksmith and the pirate queen assassin had pleased each other very much indeed.

Afterward, we lay tangled up together on the couch, covered with a soft blanket, basking in the afterglow, as well as the flames still crackling in the fireplace.

Owen drifted off to sleep with his arms wrapped around me. I put my head on his chest and let the strong, steady beat of his heart lull me to sleep as well. My last thought before I slipped into the quiet, soothing blackness was about the ren faire.

Winter's Web, The Ides of Winter, whatever you wanted to call it. The name didn't matter, only the fact that Owen and I had survived it the way we always did, just as we would survive all the challenges with Tucker, Mason, and the Circle that were looming on the horizon.

Together.

GIN BLANCO WILL RETURN

About the Author

Jennifer Estep is a *New York Times*, *USA Today*, and internationally bestselling author who prowls the streets of her imagination in search of her next fantasy idea.

Jennifer is the author of the **Elemental Assassin, Galactic Bonds, Section 47, Crown of Shards, Gargoyle Queen**, and other fantasy series. She has written more than forty books, along with numerous novellas and stories.

In her spare time, Jennifer enjoys hanging out with friends and family, doing yoga, and reading fantasy and romance books. She also watches way too much TV and loves all things related to superheroes.

For more information on Jennifer and her books, visit her website at **www.jenniferestep.com** or follow her online on Facebook, Twitter, Instagram, Amazon, BookBub, and Goodreads. You can also sign up for her newsletter.

Happy reading, everyone!

Other Books by Jennifer Estep

THE ELEMENTAL ASSASSIN SERIES
FEATURING GIN BLANCO

BOOKS
Spider's Bite
Web of Lies
Venom
Tangled Threads
Spider's Revenge
By a Thread
Widow's Web
Deadly Sting
Heart of Venom
The Spider
Poison Promise
Black Widow
Spider's Trap
Bitter Bite
Unraveled
Snared
Venom in the Veins
Sharpest Sting
Last Strand

E-NOVELLAS
Haints and Hobwebs
Thread of Death
Parlor Tricks

Kiss of Venom
Unwanted
Nice Guys Bite
Winter's Web
Heart Stings

THE GALACTIC BONDS SERIES
Only Bad Options
Only Good Enemies

THE SECTION 47 SERIES
A Sense of Danger
Sugar Plum Spies (holiday book)

THE CROWN OF SHARDS SERIES
Kill the Queen
Protect the Prince
Crush the King

THE GARGOYLE QUEEN SERIES
Capture the Crown
Tear Down the Throne
Conquer the Kingdom

THE BLACK BLADE SERIES
Cold Burn of Magic
Dark Heart of Magic
Bright Blaze of Magic

THE BIGTIME SERIES
Karma Girl
Hot Mama
Jinx
A Karma Girl Christmas (holiday story)
Nightingale
Fandemic

Made in the USA
Las Vegas, NV
20 August 2023

76343922R00139